SEX

BILLIONAIRE

BY SIERRA CARTWRIGHT

DEDICATION

Bev — what can I say? You have been with me every step of the way. Thank you. And Jennifer! Your talents are so appreciated. You both rocked this one... Twice.

Riane! Thanks for the catches and the patience. And for just being awesome. Love you!

Willow Winters, you inspired my heroine. You are so kind and fierce, talented and helpful. Life's better because I know you.

Thank you to a stellar group of fellow authors who took me under their wings: Livia Grant, Alta Hensley, Renee Rose, Rayanna Jamison. I appreciate you very much.

CHAPTER ONE

What in the actual fuck...?

Jaxon Mills froze. The woman who'd just pushed through the frosted-glass door that separated the reception area of the Quarter from the main dungeon resembled his biggest investor's only daughter.

He shook his head. It couldn't be her.

As far as he knew, Willow Henderson was tucked away at an expensive New York college earning a master's degree in social work. She sure as hell couldn't be standing in the middle of one of New Orleans's most exclusive BDSM clubs.

But holy hell, the resemblance between the two was startling, at least on the surface.

Both were tall and slender. Each time he'd seen her, Willow's hair had been in a messy bun. She dressed in soft, comfortable jeans, often with artistic rips in the fabric, and tank tops beneath long-sleeved men's shirts.

She was very different from the woman who paused to watch a submissive receiving a flogging on a nearby Saint Andrew's cross.

He lowered his sparkling water to the table as he swept his gaze over the look-alike. Her blonde hair was lit by fiery highlights and danced around her shoulders in feminine waves. She wore a black leather crop top with sexy cap sleeves that left her midriff bare. Her asymmetrical skirt was short enough to slam his imagination into dangerous territory. He pictured himself lifting the hem as she grabbed her ankles and took a deep breath before he caressed her then used his bare hand to paint her buttocks a tantalizing shade of pink. It would be even better if she was panting and screaming his name.

The woman took a step forward, perhaps to get a better view of the scene. He glanced around to see if she was with anyone. Prospective members of the Quarter were required to attend with a sponsor on their first three visits. Since she appeared to be alone, it meant she'd been here a number of times.

When the flogging ended, she turned toward the bar area. Aviana, the club's owner and respected businesswoman, had been persuaded to add one about a year ago when it was pointed out that she could open at lunchtime for members who wished to have a discreet place for business meetings. Serving lunch had been another stroke of genius—and financial gain.

Since most clubs of this nature didn't serve alcohol, it had taken her some time to establish a policy. Members or guests who imbibed at all had their hand marked with an X, which forbade play for the rest of the evening. And she had a strict two-drink rule for everyone.

The bar area was glassed in, making it much quieter than the dungeon. Jax appreciated having the opportunity to relax with a sub after a scene, providing them both a gradual transition from intensity back to the real world. At times, he'd used the space to negotiate with a new sub. On a couple of occasions, he'd even stopped by to relax after an evening out.

Aviana had decorated with a Louisiana flair. A picture of a tiger representing LSU hung from the wall, alongside an autographed New Orleans Saints football jersey, and neon signs from the thriving local brewery.

Tonight, he'd chosen his table with care. He had an excellent view of Aviana's throne, a number of the Saint Andrew's crosses, along with a few of the spanking benches. And of course, *her*. Captivated, curious, he stretched out his legs and watched her approach.

When she entered, she paused to scan the long, polished bar and the people seated there. A couple was snuggled together with their foreheads touching. Two stools were occupied by Doms without subs.

Obviously having made a decision, she walked toward the back of the space so she could sit alone, at the end of the bar, with an empty, inviting chair next to her.

About three feet away from him, she saw him and jerked to a stop, eyes wide. For a moment, their gazes locked.

Fuck it to hell. Shock, hot and white, pulsed through him.

The sexy temptress—with the parted, enticing mouth—*was* his friend's daughter. Did Brian have any idea that his only child was more than a thousand miles from school and that she liked to get her ass spanked by men she might not know?

Willow blinked, severing their connection. Instead of saying anything, she squared her shoulders and continued past him.

Jesus. What the living hell was wrong with him? He was lusting after her.

Now that Jax knew who she was, he was torn between pretending he hadn't seen her and paddling her ass himself.

If he were smart, he'd pay his bill, collect his play bag from the coat check, then go home where he could masturbate to some fantasy woman and forget he'd ever seen Willow. But he wasn't sure he could walk away, despite the risks.

The Quarter had a strict code of conduct. Movie stars, musicians, politicians, and business tycoons needed a place free from scrutiny, which made privacy Aviana's main priority. Many people opted to use a scene name, and unless there was an agreement between all parties, no one could acknowledge they knew one another outside the club. No doubt that was one of Willow's reasons for joining.

At the very least, striding over to her and turning her over his knee would guarantee a suspension of membership privileges. There a chance he'd be expelled. Since visiting the club on his rare trips to Louisiana provided a much-needed break from the grind of running his digital-media conglomerate, Jax valued his membership. So for the moment, he waited and watched, bouncing his leg with customary impatience.

She wriggled onto a barstool, exaggerating her movements — he was sure — to capture attention.

Stefan, one of the Doms at the bar — a man who was devouring his trust fund, sleeping all day, partying all night, and discarding a relationship a week — glanced toward Willow.

Jax mentally repeated the club's rules.

Willow was at least twenty-one, capable of making her own decisions. She was also free to allow a Dom to tie her up, blindfold her, flog her.

What she did was none of his business.

Still watching her, Stefan grabbed a cane from the top of the bar and tapped it against his open palm, as if in deep thought. Then he slid off his chair.

Jax snapped his back teeth together. No one was touching Willow. No one but him.

Fuck the club rules.

Shit.

The bartender slid a napkin in front of Willow. She snatched it close and shredded the edges.

"What will it be?"

Hemlock. "Something virgin." Like she wished she wasn't.

"Piña colada?"

"That sounds perfect." She tried to smile, but her facial muscles seemed frozen. "Thanks."

When she'd first started coming to the Quarter a little more than a year ago, she'd been wary, expecting to see someone who knew her father. The Quarter had a lot of members who moved in his circles, but as the months passed, she relaxed. She was comfortable flying down from grad school during breaks, and she'd become adept at navigating the intricacies of getting her needs met in a place far from home. Attending a club in New York would be easier, but after the disaster with Lawrence, she was on a break from romantic relationships. Traveling to New Orleans helped make that easier.

She risked another glance at Jaxon Mills. He was staring at her. Of all people here, why, oh why did she have to come face-to-face with the cockiest damn billionaire on the planet?

Even though he was across the room, he unnerved her, and she tore the napkin in half.

Since the moment she saw the digital marketing entrepreneur, she'd disliked him. Four years ago, Willow and her father had been among a dozen or so people who crowded into Jax's office while he recorded a video. In her naivete, she'd thought he'd be dressed in a business suit. Instead, a black T-shirt swaddled him, tight enough to show off his honed abs. Confidence and energy ignited his dark-green eyes. He spoke with rapid-fire speed, sharing strategies about how to connect on social media and build an empire like his. His presentation had been passionate and engaging, but then he'd told viewers to stop whining if they weren't enjoying the success they wanted and ordered them to get off their fucking asses and make something happen.

Shock made her drop her purse. Once the camera stopped rolling, he stood, shook hands, and high-fived another successful Jaxon Media presentation. His staff offered accolades, and he drank them in as his due, everyone bowing before the king. Who the hell behaved like that?

From her mother, Willow had inherited a different worldview, where everyone was better off working together and being supportive. Motivation was crucial. She'd been taught to offer support or lend a helping hand. But beating people up? Everything in Willow despised his self-important approach.

After his crew filed out, her father introduced them, and she forced a polite nod. Jax turned his massive focus on her. He sought her hand, and when she reluctantly accepted, electricity arced through her. The physical awareness of his power had been unwelcome and left a memorable impression on her. He repeated her name, rolling it around on his tongue, seeming to taste the syllables. Willow had never forgotten the way the he'd seared her senses.

She had the exact same reaction when he'd looked at her a few seconds ago.

Even though her appearance was dramatically different, his pupils had dilated. He recognized her. Despite the Quarter's rules, the way he leaned forward told her he intended to do something about it.

Her pulse had skidded.

Not only was the arrogant bastard at her favorite club—he was a freaking Dom. As much as she wanted to pretend that didn't matter, her submissive instincts stirred. On an elemental level, she was compelled to respond to him. What would it be like to be claimed by a man with that level of confidence? And it wasn't false bravado. A million people a day, maybe more, hung on his words, even when they were harsh. If he was as competent with a paddle as he was with a microphone...

Willow shook away the inane fantasy.

Deciding to be brave, she straightened her back in time to see a man headed her direction. He tapped a cane against his calf as he walked, and his gaze was fixed on her. *Thank God.* She could forget about Jaxon Mills and get on with her night.

"Good evening." The stranger extended his hand. "May I join you?"

"That would be —"

"No. You may not. The young lady is with me."

The atmosphere snapped around her, and she turned her head. Not that she needed to. His voice was unmistakable, as was his threatening tone. *Jax.* Of course.

Scowling, the Dom pivoted to face the taller and much more muscled Jax. In the years since she'd seen him, he'd gotten leaner. He wore his trademark black T-shirt and black boots, but tonight he'd switched out jeans for tailored black trousers.

Apparently he was not friends with a razor, and his hair was longer than she remembered. Willow twisted her fingers together to fight off the ridiculous urge to run them through his thick locks, maybe muss them to make him seem less formidable.

"She appears to be alone," the Dom said.

"Ask her." Jax shrugged.

Willow exhaled. They were having a ridiculous territorial battle, as if she was some sort of prize.

The bartender placed her drink on the remnants of the napkin. "Everything okay?"

She nodded a silent lie. Nothing about Jax was okay.

"The club code word is *red*," he reminded her. "Use it and I'll send both of these men home." The bartender directed his gaze at the Dom then at Jax.

"I'll be right here." He folded his arms and remained in place.

"What's it going to be?" Jax asked, voice easy, apparently confident of her response.

He loved being the center of attention. And in the end, he would win. All he had to do was call her dad. Then the wrath of hell would descend. Worse, if he told her mother, the gentle Andrea would collapse in a pile of disappointment. After all, Willow was their only child. For the first ten years of their marriage, Brian and Andrea had tried to have children. She'd spent agonizing years not conceiving, and when she finally did, she endured two miscarriages. To say they'd do anything to protect Willow from the world was an understatement. She sighed. With a smile so fake her teeth ached, she turned toward Stefan. "I'm with him."

"Good night, Stefan." Using his impressive frame, Jax nudged the other man aside to take possession of the seat next to her.

"Sorry to have interrupted." With a firm scowl in place, Stefan nodded.

"Give my regards to Leah."

"Fuck you, Mills."

It took several seconds for Stefan to walk off. Then the bartender gave her another pointed look. "I'm here until eleven if you need anything."

"Thank you." She appreciated knowing the club's staff and monitors paid attention to every interaction, no matter how important the member.

He rapped a knuckle on the bar top before leaving to pour a beer requested by another customer.

All of a sudden, she was alone with Jax. "Who's Leah?"

"His girlfriend."

"Oh my God." She pulled her straw from the piña colada and stabbed it back in. "I didn't know. I hate cheaters." After being the one duped, it was especially painful. She'd never be a participant in hurting another woman.

"I figured it might make a difference to you."

It did. She supposed she should be grateful to Jax for saving her from making a mistake. "Is his girlfriend a submissive?"

Jax lifted a shoulder in a noncommittal shrug. He sat close enough that she inhaled his scent. Power spiced with arrogance. Jaxon Mills was a man who took what he wanted.

"Are you?" His approving gaze lingered on her.

"Am I...what?"

"Submissive?"

Even though she didn't want to have a reaction other than disdain for him, her traitorous heart rapped out a dangerous sexual tattoo. "We're not having this conversation."

"No?"

Desperate for a distraction, she took a big drink of the nonalcoholic piña colada. The freezing cold gave her an instant headache at the back of her skull. "You think you're being a hero, but I don't need someone to cockblock for me." If only he knew how ridiculous that idea was. For her, BDSM had nothing to do with sex. She loved impact play. There was a lick of pain, followed by a rush of pleasure. Enough of it vanquished all other thoughts from her mind, sweeping away her worries and helping her lock away stress for days. Scening was better than a hot bath or a kick-ass cocktail. It was as meditative as it was restorative. And she wasn't about to let him stand in her way. "You can go away now."

"I'm afraid I'm not going to be able to do that, princess."

CHAPTER TWO

Damn him. His words, flat and emotionless, took her breath, even though she should have expected them. "Look..." Willow shoved away her drink. "There's no reason for you to behave this way."

"Which way?"

"As if..." *You own me.* He sat close to her. Too close for her comfort. A little more distance would make it easier for her to think. She desperately needed that, because right now, she wanted to be across his lap, pretending to be fighting to get away as he paddled her. And of course, he was so much bigger and stronger. She could struggle all she wanted, and he'd be able to subdue her.

Scandalized by her own thoughts, she inched back in her seat. Instantly she regretted it. The friction shot arousal through her.

"You're the daughter of my biggest investor. A man who's a trusted adviser. Someone I consider a friend."

Pampered and protected. Unspoken, those words hung between them.

When she was at college in Houston, he'd assigned men to watch over her. He'd refused to use the term *bodyguards*, but that was exactly who they were. Once she'd realized he was having her followed, they'd had the biggest argument ever. Without telling her father, she'd applied for a scholarship to graduate school in New York and found a part-time job working in a crisis center so she didn't have to touch her trust fund. Even though her mother had cried for days, Willow had remained resolute. She loved her parents dearly, but she needed to escape Houston and find her own place in the world. "Club rules prevent you from telling him. Your membership could be revoked."

"I respect confidentiality. I would never betray that."

"Good." Willow waved a dismissive hand. "I'm here to enjoy myself, and that's what I plan to do. You've done your good deed. I hope you're happy with yourself." She slid from the barstool. "I hope you enjoy your evening." Another lie. "No. That's not true. After the way you ruined my night, I hope yours sucks."

"Wait." Jax's word was as forceful as any pair of handcuffs, and the command in it rooted her to the spot.

"Sit back down." The words were lethal. More than ever, she understood how he enthralled audiences.

An internal battle waged in her — obedience to a Dominant who turned her on, and an instinctive urge to flee from an asshole who made her tremble.

"Please."

Anything but an irresistible entreaty. Willow wrapped her arms around her midriff.

"I want to talk."

"I have news for you, Mr. Bigshot Internet Star. Communication is a two-way street. I know thousands of people hang on your every word and worship your advice like gospel, but I'm not one of them." She was already so far in that she decided to go for broke. "In fact, I find you and your approach offensive."

"Do you?"

Damn his dark soul, he grinned.

Those might have been the wrong words. Rather than offended, he seemed challenged and invigorated.

"Please sit," he repeated.

The bartender meandered closer, putting away wineglasses, then leaning back to adjust the gold garter he wore around his biceps.

"No more threats?"

"I never threatened you, Willow."

God. The way he said her name — breaking it into two syllables and trailing off in a whisper of seduction that shot rockets through her. He wasn't just dominant. He was dangerous. "You'd have to promise to zip your mouth shut and listen to me too." She marveled at her defiance of a man wielding so much power over her life.

"Agreed." He extended his hand.

She stared at it. The one time they'd touched, she carried his psychic impression for days. This time, she was smarter. She ignored him and lifted herself back onto the stool.

He lifted one eyebrow in a mock salute.

Once she was as comfortable as she could be with him crowding her space, she reached for her drink.

He flicked a glance at her hand, looking for the X, she guessed.

"You came here to scene," he said.

"Nothing gets by you, does it, Sherlock Holmes."

He signaled for the bartender and ordered a club soda. "Look. Can we have a truce?"

Not with the way nerves zapped through her veins.

"You're a sub."

It was a statement more than a question. She'd had these discussions with numerous men, and none of them had disturbed her as much as he did. "I'm more of a bottom." She swirled her straw around the inside of her glass.

Surprising her, he waited for her to continue. Aware that her words might someday be used against her, she proceeded with care. "I'm into kink, but not on a full-time basis."

She paused while the bartender delivered Jax's drink. Her body language must have changed since the man wasn't watching them as intently as he had before. After ensuring they didn't need anything else, he walked off.

Jax ignored his glass in favor of studying her. "Go on."

"I don't want to be in a submissive partnership, but I like..." How the hell was she supposed to admit this to one of her dad's friends? "I like going out, and I crave impact play." She took a drink that she didn't want while she finished her thought. "It sets me free."

"Impact by itself? Or sensation, such as clamps? Or a Wartenberg wheel?"

Willow shivered. Not because she was scared, but because the idea of the pinwheel of tiny metal spikes pricking into her skin intrigued her.

"Ice? Heat?"

With other tops, she'd negotiated implements, discussed her pain tolerance, agreed on safe words. No one else had asked about torturing her in other ways. "I don't know." She stared into her drink.

"Tell me what things you have explored."

"I've told you everything I'm going to." She brought her chin up. If she didn't shut up this moment, she might confess she was fantasizing about him rubbing a piece of ice over her clit. "Why are *you* here?"

"I have a couple of clubs that I enjoy. The Retreat in Houston. Another in Boston, but this is my favorite. I had a meeting...nearby."

Breath rushed from her lungs. His slight hesitation omitted a ton of information, specifics that her mind filled in. She glanced at his right hand. As she expected he wore a gold ring. Though he wasn't close enough to make out all the details, emeralds winked in the overhead light, and she knew those were meant to be the eyes of an owl. Her heart plummeted.

Like her father, Jax was a member of the Titans, one of the oldest secret societies in the United States. The organization had thousands of members, a who's-who list of people from all over the world. The annual dues were astronomical, and the wait list to join was years long. The Titans, officially known as the Zeta Society, owned an estate on the banks of the Mississippi River. As a child, she'd visited a couple of times with her mom and dad, but never during the yearly meeting as nonmembers were banned from attending.

The Zetas did a fair amount of charity work, and they'd saved a magnificent historical home from demolition. Still, she chafed at the extreme waste of money that could be funneled into better purposes.

"So, you know." It wasn't a guess. It was a statement.

"Yes."

"You sound disapproving."

His membership explained a lot. How he'd gotten some big-name clients and achieved superstar success at such an early age. Titans helped other Titans.

Then she took a drink to escape the obvious. He would never have been admitted to the society without merit. Only descendants of founding members received a legacy admission. He'd earned a seat at the table. "I'm studying for my master's in social work, Jax." She chose her words with care, as he did, avoiding the mention of the Zetas. "I'd like to see people allot their resources differently."

"Ah." He nodded. "There's only one way to do good in the world? Your way?"

She brought her chin up. "I don't berate people."

"Is that how you see it? You don't think some people need a metaphoric kick in the pants?"

Willow gave him a great big, fake smile. "Present company included?"

He lifted his glass in a toast to her.

"And no. I think if people have a compelling reason, passion, they will move forward of their own volition."

"Is that true?" His words held more interest than challenge, making her consider what she'd said. "Or are individuals different?" he persisted. "Do we each respond to different stimuli?"

Her breath caught as he looked at her barely covered body.

"Pain. Sensation. Pleasure. All of them tied together in an inextricable knot so that you don't know where one ends and the other begins?"

They were no longer talking about social consciousness.

"Is it possible that you're right, but that my way works also?"

To his credit, he didn't flaunt the fact that people thought he held the holy grail to success. Because she cared about helping people through their struggles, she answered him thoughtfully. "I'm concerned with life balance more than you seem to be. You're constantly talking about pushing, focusing on work to the exclusion of everything else. People need time to pause, to reflect. Think about positive things. Spend time with family and friends. Socialize. Connect. Laugh. Maybe ride a bike, but indulge in some fun. *That's* what makes life worth living."

"Maybe you should watch more and judge less."

She blinked. She looked for the best in people and encouraged them to explore it. "That's unkind."

"Perhaps it's true."

Beneath his penetrating glare, she fidgeted.

"I presented a commencement address for a high school in a disadvantaged area last year. Look it up."

She studied him through narrowed eyes, unwilling to acknowledge that maybe she didn't know everything about him. On the other hand, the fact that he was still here rather than leaving her the hell alone to get her needs met was proof enough of his cocksure attitude.

"Do you play in the dungeon? Or do you prefer *Rue Sensuelle*?"

He'd switched subjects so fast that it took her a minute to catch up. "I'm sorry?"

"When you scene, where do you like to play?"

The Quarter had two floors, and the first was set up in an interesting horseshoe shape. The dungeon area was a square, and beyond that was another play area for people who preferred a little more solitude. On the far side lay *Rue Sensuelle* — or Kinky Avenue as most members called it. There were a number of different settings, separated by partitions. Each was furnished to appeal to a particular fetish. From what she'd heard, there was a schoolroom, a pair of stocks, and a Victorian chamber, complete with a brass bed. There was even supposed to be an examination table. The idea of being strapped to that terrified her.

He remained silent, waiting for her answer.

"I..." Why was this so difficult with him? Willow had negotiated with a dozen different Doms. She didn't have to answer. Yet she wanted to. "Typically in the main area. I like the Saint Andrew's cross or a spanking bench."

"Which is your preference?"

"The Saint Andrew's cross. It's" — *emotionally safer* — "less personal, I suppose."

"I'm guessing you like a flogging, then?"

"Actually..."

He leaned toward her, ensnaring her in his massive focus. For that moment, no one existed but her. And that gave her the courage she needed. "I haven't had a lot of bare-bottom spankings." Her body temperature increased, and she knew scarlet had flooded her cheeks.

"You'd like one?"

"From you? No! I wasn't asking."

He grinned, and his features transformed. For a moment, he looked less hostile, more human. Inviting and approachable. Feminine instinct whispered that she needed to be extra cautious. A charming Jaxon Mills might prove devastating.

"Over the knee? Or tied to a spanking bench?"

Either. Both. What the hell was wrong with her?

"When you make an arrangement with a Dom, what do you tell him?"

She crossed her legs and took the opportunity to tighten her pelvic muscles. Even though she didn't want to be, Willow was horny for this overbearing man.

"I'm waiting."

"Of course, I let him know that my safe word is *red*, like the club's. And I use yellow for slow. And absolutely no physical penetration."

"That includes no ass play?"

She shook her head so fast that her hair swung around her face. "Not ever."

"Is your hypothetical Dom allowed to touch your clit?"

His question sucked the air from her lungs. Her father's *friend* was asking this? And worse, she was going to answer. "I've never said yes to that before."

"But you'd be open to it?"

Am I? She glanced at his ridiculously big hand. His finger would be rough against her skin. She tried to speak, but no words emerged.

"Would he be allowed to wedge your panties between your legs and use the fabric to get you off?"

She grabbed her drink and gulped down enough that she coughed.

"I'll take that as a yes." A wry laugh wrapped around his words.

Willow slammed her glass back onto the napkin much harder than she'd intended to.

"Do you like to orgasm during a scene? Or do you just like to get lost?"

"Lost," she replied. "I don't think I'm able to."

He leaned forward. "Can you clarify what you mean?"

What was it about him that invited her to reveal more than she wanted to? With other Doms, she'd drawn the line at penetration, and they'd agreed. No one had asked for more information. "Well, I mean... I never have. Orgasmed at a club."

"Has anyone else used sensation play with you?"

Her nerves were shattered. Even though she didn't intend to, she plucked the straw from the glass just so she had something to toy with. "No."

"Is it something you want to try?"

"Maybe. I mean, we're talking hypothetically, right? It would depend on a few things, such as whether the right Dom asked." She was leading a dangerous dance. Flirting, considering. Despite the warnings bouncing around inside her head, she couldn't stop herself from wanting to make a mistake with him.

"What toys do you like?"

"Nothing too intense. Paddles are okay. Hairbrushes, wooden spoons." With other Doms, they were inanimate objects, but when she spoke with him, she couldn't help but imagine him holding the implements. Round and round, she twisted the straw.

"A devil's tail?"

"I haven't tried one."

"You might like it. A tiny bite, maybe a bit more. Can be used with extreme precision and in tight, even intimate places. The red lines it leaves behind are rather appealing."

"But…"

"Tell me what you're thinking."

"I like the way those implements cover a wider area. There's a"—she sought out a description that made sense, something that was complicated since she hadn't thought it through herself—"I guess an *oomph* factor. The impact forces my body forward. It's an instinctive reaction. And the way it hurts, and the marks…" Thinking about it left her needy. She had to scene tonight. Had to.

He nodded slowly, taking in her words. "Since you've mentioned the Saint Andrew's cross, I'm also assuming you're familiar with a flogger."

"Yes. But heavier ones. The way the falls wrap around my sides…they cover so much area, you know. So many impact points, things happening all at the same time. It's a lot to take in. Too much, even."

"You like that."

"Yeah." She breathed out, wondering if he sensed her dreaminess.

"Anything else you want me to know?"

Dare she? "My favorite is a—"she cleared her throat—"an open hand." His. Jaxon Mills was a commanding presence. At six-two, maybe six-three, he was taller than most men she knew. No doubt, he was capable of delivering what she wanted, maybe better than anyone else had. The question was, would he?

"So it's the impact? Maybe the sound?"

She met his gaze. He understood her. "And the intimacy. There's nothing between me and my Dom."

"It's your lucky night, Willow. I have a few paddles in my bag. And I've been told I have rather strong hands. And there's nothing I'd like more than having you turned over my lap with your bottom bared."

Jax plucked the straw from her nerveless fingers. The melty coconut liquid dribbled over the glossy bar surface as he returned it to the glass. "Now it's my turn to tell you what I look for when I top a woman."

He had demands of his own? The realization shouldn't surprise her. Of course there had to be a catch. "Such as?"

"I want her naked. No clothes between us."

"Which means a private room." On the first floor, certain protocols had to be followed. Patrons had to wear panties, no matter how skimpy. And women's nipples had to be covered in some way. Many people chose electrical tape or a sheer bra, even pasties. But upstairs, a place she'd never visited, the only rule was the enforcement of a safe word. She'd heard stories of things that happened in those rooms, and she assumed most were tall tales.

Willow had never been naked with a man. That she hadn't already stopped Jax stunned her. What kind of spell did he have over her?

Unaware of what he was doing to her insides, he continued. "My rules…I agree to give my sub what she wants and honor her limits and safe word. But within her parameters, I set the pace." His tone, which had been even, roughened. He captured her chin. "The bottom is not in charge."

Lust rocketed through her. She cleared her throat, trying to convince herself this was an ordinary negotiation with an ordinary man.

He released his hold on her. Until then, she hadn't realized she'd stopped breathing.

Seizing any opportunity to dance away from the trouble—the inevitability—that she was steaming toward, she tried for a diversion. "I got distracted earlier. I asked why you visit clubs. I mean besides the obvious of telling people what to do."

He gave a quick smile. Part of her enjoyed their verbal sparring.

"Like you, I find impact play rewarding. As you said, connection with others is important. Quality over quantity." He kept her gaze ensnared. "Despite what you think you know, I believe focus is more important than actual hours worked. I can accomplish more in five hours than other people can in ten."

He wasn't bragging, and she knew it.

"I work out every morning. Sleep six to seven hours." More quietly, sensually, so she had to strain to hear him, he added, "I like being in charge."

"Why doesn't that surprise me?"

"Pleasing a woman is its own reward. So very satisfying."

"And you get to do it without any commitments or the complications that come with a relationship."

"You said that. I didn't."

She narrowed her eyes. "You don't have a girlfriend or wife waiting for you at home?"

"No. In case I wasn't clear, I don't cheat."

In fact, she wasn't sure she'd ever heard of him being in a relationship. The way he spoke to her calmed her. Slowly, the rest of her resistance dissipated.

"Let's be clear with each other, Willow. You want to indulge in some impact play and lose yourself. I'll do my damnedest to please you. One more thing." He paused for a moment. "If you want to get your needs met tonight, it will be with me and no other man. Am I clear?"

He captured her gaze. It would be smarter to go back to her hotel. Scening with a man as forceful as him would be madness. Already, he'd made an indelible claim on her, and she was far too smart to allow this to go any further.

Wasn't she?

CHAPTER THREE

In the course of his thirty-two years on the planet, Jax had taken a lot of risks…all of them calculated. He'd also made a handful of unfortunate dumbass decisions. But until now, not a damn one of them had been made by his dick.

He shouldn't be thinking about taking his friend's daughter upstairs to a private room, baring her ass, then spanking it. Yet that was precisely what he planned to do.

Some fucking hero I am.

"What will it be, Willow?"

When she spoke, her words resonated with confidence, bringing him to his knees. "Yes. I want to play with you."

He eased off the barstool and offered his hand. This time, she took it. He leaned forward so that his mouth was near her ear before he said, "I'm giving you one last chance to run."

The desire in his eyes made her shiver. "Are you planning to hurt me?"

"Very much so. In the exact ways you want."

"Then why are you warning me away?" Breathlessness weaved through her words, curiosity and wariness mixing.

"For a million reasons. Especially because I respect your father."

She angled her chin and delivered a ferocious scowl. He schooled himself not to respond.

"You picked a fine time to discover some integrity, Jax."

He imagined she hoped to offend him. "If I may continue…?" He didn't wait for permission before going on, this time with steel in his words. "This *is* a matter of integrity. I don't care whether you think I have any or not. Without Brian's belief in me, Jaxon Media wouldn't be where it is today. I owe him a debt. If we go forward, you'll be mine."

"I don't belong to anyone."

"That's why I'm offering you one last chance to tell me to go to hell. If you don't, you might regret it."

"Your conscience is annoying."

All his life, Jax had avoided entanglements. He'd seen what had happened to his dad, after his mother had given up, abandoning her kid and the man who'd knocked her up and refused to marry her. His father had drunk too much, struggled to keep a job after the coal mine closed up, brought home too damn many women, some who hadn't known he had a kid. Jax learned use a can opener when he was four, the stove when he was five. At nine, a teacher had recommended him for a summer camp, the first really good thing that had happened to him. He'd gotten out of the hellhole of a trailer where he lived, and he'd been served both breakfast and lunch every day. Best of all, he'd learned how to record videos. He'd attended some acting sessions and received voice coaching. Once the little light on a camera started blinking, he turned into a different person — someone he wanted to be. He thrived on the attention his videos garnered. It became his obsession, the thing that helped him hang on.

He began teaching others what he knew, running their sites, earning money and hoarding it beneath his shabby mattress so his dad didn't find it. Jax was fifteen when his father discovered the cash. He'd called his son vile names before beating the shit out of him.

With a black eye and broken ribs, Jax had grabbed his camera and the forty bucks that his old man had missed. The screen door had slammed behind him. Doubled over, his father shouting curses from their rickety front porch, Jax limped away, and he hadn't ever looked back.

Every day, he got in front of his first love, his savior — the camera — and recorded something. It was as essential to him as breathing. Willow was right. A lot of his words were fucking harsh. Too bad. So was life. He had no time for coddling. Grinding was the only way to beat the odds stacked against success. It meant pushing all the time, and all the time, he reminded himself and his subscribers of that.

Through the years that he'd fought through poverty and hunger, he never lost sight of his goal. Security. For that reason, he'd avoided entanglements.

Until now, he'd never been tempted.

Until Willow.

"What's it to be?" he asked. If she agreed, he was stepping onto a forbidden path. And there'd be no turning back for either of them. "Frustration or satisfaction?"

"No matter what, I'm afraid I'm going to end up disliking you."

No doubt. Right now, he had a lot of power. "It's a risk I'm prepared to take."

For a long time, she studied him, contemplating.

"Are you at least a halfway decent Dom?"

"Am I as...?" His mouth twitched. "I've never had any complaints."

"If you're going to ruin my life, you'd better make it worth my while."

"Princess, you have my word that you won't go back to school unsatisfied." He extended an inviting hand toward her.

With a sigh, she pressed her palm against his.

"So brave." *So foolish.*

She slipped from the stool and very nearly into his arms.

Fuck if he didn't want her there.

Together, they walked back to the main reception area. Aviana wasn't near the podium, but Trinity was. He knew very little about the woman, and he suspected she liked it that way. Her hair was a sleek hot-pink bob that fell over her face, often shielding her completely. Her eyes were violet, a color that didn't exist in nature. And always, she wore a tight-fitting catsuit, either vinyl or PVC.

She greeted them with a smile. "Something I can help you with, sir?"

"We'd like a private room."

Trinity brushed back her hair and tucked it behind her ear. "You're consenting, ma'am?"

Had everyone heard about the minor altercation at the bar?

"Yes." Willow nodded. "Thank you for asking, Trinity."

Trinity grabbed a book from a shelf in the podium, then logged them in. "Room five."

"My lucky number."

"Please check back when you're done."

After a promise to do so, he led Willow toward the coat-check room to collect his toy bag.

While they waited, Willow turned toward him. "Five's your lucky number?"

"Yeah."

"Why?"

"I earned five bucks for first video I shot. Kid at school was skateboarding, he wanted to see himself."

"Hustling even back then."

"Five led to fifty. Then five hundred." And broken bones, but an unshakable determination.

The clerk returned with his bag. Jax gave a tip, then looked at Willow. "Ready?"

"Yes."

Her breathing had evened out, letting him know that she'd moved past her frustration—at least for the moment. He liked seeing this relaxed side of her.

They pushed through the frosted-glass door into the dungeon and were swallowed by the pulsing sounds and sights. "How often do you attend?"

"I'm not going to answer that."

Which meant it was pretty damn often, something he intended to put an immediate stop to. He tightened his grip on his bag. Another valuable lesson. Never ask a question unless you wanted to hear the answer.

Near a Saint Andrew's cross, her steps slowed, and she touched his forearm. "Can we watch for a moment?"

"Of course." It was the first time she'd touched him without his prompting. At this point, he'd gift wrap the moon and offer it to her on a star.

A pretty submissive was secured with her back to the X-shaped frame. She was blindfolded, and dozens of clothespins pinched tiny pieces of skin. Her Dom was flicking them off one at a time with a crop, each stroke making her scream in agony.

Surprising him, Willow's mouth was parted and her eyes were glazed. He had no doubt she would enjoy sensation play, even though she hadn't indulged before.

When all of the clips had clattered to the concrete floor, Willow exhaled, and she dropped her hand. There was so much he wanted to introduce her to, so many places they could go together. "Are you ready to go on?"

They walked through the dungeon and pushed open the door leading to the U-shaped part of the Quarter and the stairs to the second floor. It was much quieter. Much more intimate.

When they were halfway up, they paused at the landing. From here it was possible to survey the entire club. The dungeon was a hive of activity, thumping in time to the music.

Two rooms were occupied in Kinky Avenue. In one, a sub wearing a thong and pasties was fastened into the stocks, and her gaze was fixed on the Dom in front of her as he sorted through his collection of canes.

"Perfect for voyeurs," Jax said.

"Is that one of your kinks?"

"From time to time, yes. I enjoy participating, but I also admit I love watching a woman surrender.

I get a kick from all of her reactions, joy, fear." Willow's head was tipped back. Her hazel eyes were wide, and her wariness had been replaced with interest, stroking his already massive ego. "I'm particularly looking forward to watching the striptease you're going to perform for me."

Color danced onto her face. For a woman who was bold enough to visit the Quarter and ask strange men to flog her, she had an air of innocence about her. He appreciated the fact that she had a no-penetration rule. It meant he didn't have to look at every Dom with suspicion and find out whose ass he needed to kick. "Have you seen enough?"

She swallowed. "Yes. I'm ready."

They continued up the stairs. Tore, Aviana's most trusted dungeon monitor, stood at the entrance to the private rooms, arms folded across his massive chest. Like all other monitors at the club, his black vest was adorned with a gold fleur-de-lis.

"Monitors check on the scenes from time to time," Tore informed them.

"Thank you." Willow nodded.

After stroking his beard, he stepped aside.

Jax rested his fingertips against her back, on her exposed skin, right above the waistband of her skirt. She hissed in a breath. And like each time they touched, sexual force pulsed through him—something alive, something he wanted to mainline.

At the entrance to their room, she waited for him open the door before preceding him inside.

The walls were painted a neutral color, which left the spanking bench as the main focus. Pleasing him, she went to it and trailed her hand across the top.

After placing his bag on the side table that was made from surgical steel, Jax dragged a chair to the center of the room. "Talk to me, Willow, at any time. You won't be gagged." He paused. *"This time."* As certain as the sun would rise, he would dominate this innocent again.

Her tiny gasp pleased him—fear wrapped in a gentle plea.

"Now for the show you're going to put on for me. Please remove your shoes." He sat and steepled his hands in front of him.

He expected some hesitation. To his delight, she showed none. She wanted this as much as he did.

With her gaze on him, watching his reactions, she lifted one foot and tugged off the black stiletto. She had exquisite balance, and she had taken his words about a striptease to heart. The shoe fell to the floor with a sensuous thud.

She repeated the process with the second shoe before scooping them up and tucking them beneath his chair.

He inhaled her fresh scent. It reminded him of spring. Rebirth and hope. Over the years of being surrounded by people as ambitious as he was, she provided a respite he hadn't known he needed.

Willow returned to where she'd been standing and reached behind her to lower the zipper on her skirt. She let go of the leather all at once, sending it swishing past her hips.

She stood before him in a T-back thong, the barest scrap of lace covering her pussy.

Rather than revealing that bit of herself, she moved closer to him.

What in the fuck was she thinking?

She straddled his knees, not lowering herself, but leaning her upper body toward him. "You asked for a striptease, Sir."

What in the fuck had *he* been thinking?

Willow skimmed her hands up her ribs to take hold of her crop top. As she pulled it up, she gyrated her body. His cock swelled, pushing hard against his zipper. When she'd said no penetration, he'd had no idea how difficult that might prove to be.

She dropped the garment on top of his head in a brash, sassy move he admired.

Jesus. She was sexy. Her breasts were plumper than he'd thought, and her dusky nipples were large, pink, and already erect.

"Damn it, Willow. You'd better tell me you've never done this before." He'd never experienced jealousy before. And now, with her, it had happened twice. It destroyed him, a hated, all-consuming emotion, blurring his vision.

As if she understood how much this mattered to him, she cradled his head. "You're the first."

"And the last." He dragged her against him, patience at an end. "Give me your breasts, princess."

"Yes." She lowered herself onto his lap, her heat against his crotch.

Obediently she cupped one of her breasts in her palms. Driving him wild, she rubbed a nipple on his face.

He laved the swollen nub with his tongue. Her answering moan drove him on. He sucked her flesh into his mouth, increasing the pressure until she clung to him. "Rub out an orgasm." He pinched her free nipple while he continued to torment the first. One of these days, he'd attach half a dozen clips to each of her breasts and take great pleasure in flicking them off.

An innocent seductress with no idea how powerful she was, she moved against him, moaning, then whimpering when he sucked harder.

When he sensed she was close, he switched to her other breast and squeezed the damp one hard between his thumb and forefinger.

"Oh Jax..."

His cock surged in response to her plaintive sigh, giving her something even harder to grind against. Even through her thong and his slacks, he felt her heat. She was exquisite.

Her motions grew more frantic, and he responded, pinching and sucking harder.

Less than a minute later, she tipped her head back, hair falling in wild abandon as she screamed. He'd been with plenty of women before, but none as unselfconscious as her.

He eased off the pressure on her nipples by degrees so that the blood didn't return with a painful wave. There'd be plenty of time to torment her later.

She collapsed against him and dropped her head onto his shoulder. He held her, stroked her skin, and murmured, "You're perfect." Jax always provided aftercare for women he scened with, but he'd never enjoyed it this much.

"That was…" When she finally roused, she flattened her palm on his chest and pushed herself back. She wore a self-satisfied smile. "You're…"

He filled in the silence. "An amazing Dom?

"How does your head fit inside a room?"

He waited for her to speak again.

"You're pretty darn good."

"That sounds tepid. I don't do tepid." He circled her tiny wrist with his fingers and returned her grin. "Challenge accepted."

"I was hoping you'd say that."

"You're bewitching." He dug his free hand into her hair to pull back her head so that she read the hungry intent in his eyes. Jax had never been hotter for a woman. "Time for your first spanking."

"First?"

CHAPTER FOUR

A tremor rocked through Willow, feeding desire. Discovering impact play had liberated her in a way nothing else had. At school, at her parents' home, expectations were lovingly heaped on her. But once she entered a dungeon, she unleashed her inhibitions. She asked for what she wanted and savored each moment. She refused to allow Jax's threat to unburden his soul and admit he'd despoiled Brian Henderson's daughter to ruin her evening. Right now, she craved her temporary Dom's touch.

When he drove away Stefan, she'd been pissed. But her breasts ached in a way they never had before. Other Doms were competent and had given her what she asked for, yet Jax had taken the time to notice what she liked in someone else's scene. That he'd given her an orgasm before they'd really started made any future consequences worth it.

"We'll begin with my hand."

Her favorite. He had been paying attention.

"You're going to like it." Certainty made his voice rough. "Ask for it."

"Please, Jax." Since he still gripped her hair and her wrist, she recognized his strength. Terrifying. Delicious. "Spank me."

His eyes flared.

He released her suddenly. Within seconds, she was over his lap, breath whooshing from her lungs. *Yes.* She touched her fingers to the smooth wood floor as anticipation unfurled. He stroked her thighs and buttocks in a warm-up that she'd be fine with skipping.

His first few smacks were gentle, and she shifted restlessly, rising onto her toes and all but pressing her buttocks into his hands.

He chuckled. "I told you I'm in charge."

The next smack blazed. She went rigid. It damn well hurt. And she exhaled in relief now that he'd established his dominance.

"My speed, princess."

"Yes, yes. Your speed, Jax."

Point made, he continued the spanking in a rhythmic, ritualistic way. He covered her skin with kisses of pain, rubbing some away while exploiting others.

Once her brain acknowledged he was trustworthy, she closed her eyes in surrender.

The spanking was the best of her life. He went on forever, holding her tight to keep her in position and making her cry out even as she sighed her satisfaction.

Her mind flew. Worries and stress floated away, as if wrapped in gossamer strands.

She wasn't even aware that he'd stopped until his voice penetrated her haze.

"Come back, Willow." He snapped his fingers near her ear, and she shook her head to clear the pink fuzz coating her brain.

After helping her to sit up, he cradled her against him. "You entered subspace?" he asked, tucking wild strands of hair behind her ear.

"I…" She tried to hold up her head, but it lolled onto his shoulder. "Uhm." She giggled.

"Just from that?"

"It doesn't happen all the time." She drew in a lazy breath filled with his sexy scent. It might be reckless, but she didn't want to ever move. "I like it when it does."

"That can be dangerous with the wrong Dom. You could get seriously hurt, Willow. I won't permit it."

Her ass was sore, but in a wonderful way. Because of the way he'd warmed her up, she wouldn't bruise, even though she wished he'd left marks she could admire for the next few days.

"Are you listening to me?" His tone was a whiplash, forcing her to look at him.

"What?"

With patience, he repeated himself. "Subspace can be dangerous if you're with the wrong Dom."

"But I'm with the right one."

"Holy Christ."

She smiled and relaxed against him, enjoying his struggle. It might not be nice of her, but she liked knowing she annoyed the sexy billionaire.

Within a few minutes, the objects in the room came into focus. She took a deep breath and sat up, instantly regretting the loss of his comfort and body heat. "That was nice." She could have stayed snuggled against him forever.

"Is that all it was?"

"No! I mean that's good, right?"

"Do you know your name?"

"What?" She frowned at him. "Of course."

"Then you are correct. I haven't done my job satisfactorily. Please go to the table and unpack my bag."

Intrigued, she scampered off his lap to unzip his bag. She pulled out sanitizing wipes, a bottle of water, cuffs, clamps, and a gag that he'd said he wouldn't use on her. Reaching deeper, she extracted a blindfold and the terrifying-looking Wartenberg wheel. When she saw his paddles, she knew he was the Dom for her. One of them looked as if it was supposed to be used for ping-pong. Another was wooden with terrifying holes drilled in it. Unable to help herself, she stuck her fingers through a couple of the small round openings.

"I guessed you would like that one."

"It looks evil."

"Which is exactly why I assumed you'd be drawn to it."

She continued on, laying out each item with precise spacing. By the time she was finished, she'd removed another paddle, along with a tawse, a small flogger, and a dragon's tail.

"How brave are you?"

Willow's glance went to the vicious paddle. She was desperate to play with all his toys. One night wouldn't be enough. Her thoughts reeled when she realized that meant she wanted to see him again.

"Bring it to me."

She picked it up by the handle and carried it in her upturned palms.

"Thank you."

The note of approval in his voice as he accepted the offering heated her insides.

"Do you need me to tie you to the bench?"

"No. I give myself over to my Dom. It's never been a struggle for me to remain in place. But if it's something that turns you on, it's not a limit for me."

"Another time, perhaps."

Her breath froze. His casual mention of a future meant his thoughts mirrored hers. She didn't dare voice how much she hoped that came true.

"Please bend over the bench."

Once she was in position, he asked, "Do I have your permission to touch you over your panties?"

"I thought you wanted me naked."

"A change of heart."

Frowning, she lifted her head to look back over her shoulder.

A small smile toyed with his lips. "Safer for both of us."

The knowledge that he wanted her was an aphrodisiac.

"I'm asking for your consent."

She'd been so consumed with thinking about him that she'd forgotten to answer. "Yes. You may touch my clit through my panties."

Once again he warmed her up before picking up the paddle. Willow closed her eyes and exhaled, pushing away all stray thoughts so she could focus on the heady mix of pleasure and pain.

He worked his way up and down each thigh and covered each buttock with light taps, and even those were worse than most of the leather paddles she'd experienced. He started over, repeating his pattern but with a few random, unexpected strikes.

She was breathless when he grabbed her panties and yanked them higher, wedging them in her pussy. The sensation was sharp, in such a good way. She wanted to come already.

"You're wet."

There was no need to answer.

He rubbed her clit, and it couldn't have seared more if he'd touched her bare skin.

She pushed back, silently begging for more. Instead of giving it to her, Jax moved his hand to the middle of her back. He kept a physical connection between them as he blazed her skin. The wood whistled through the air with each strike. Her whimpers turned to sobs from the force of the release he gave her.

When it was over, he helped her to stand. Her knees wobbled, and she grabbed his forearm for support. She caught sight of them in the mirror. Her hair was a mess, her eyes were wide, and tears streaked her face. Her ass was red, and a few of the lines were deep enough to linger.

Then their gazes met. He looked at her with possession and hunger in his narrowed eyes. "No man but me will ever do this to you."

"Jax," she whispered, turning to him, only him. "I need you to make love to me."

Aching to bury his cock deep inside her and drive away the hunger threatening to devour them both, Jax folded her into his arms and held her until she stopped shaking.

"Will you?"

He eased back to hold her head between his hands. "No. I can't, Willow, as much as I want to." Honor was the only thing that provided him with the strength to deny her.

He'd paddled her hard, and when he helped her up, the sight of the tear tracks staining her face told him she'd been lost in her pleasure. If he fucked her now, he'd be taking advantage of her vulnerable state. But if she asked again outside of the club? He would never be able to resist.

"You're refusing me?" Her voice was soft with rejection.

"I'm trying to be a hero," he countered.

"Don't."

"Fuck, princess. Have some mercy. I'd do damn near anything to please you. But I agreed to your rules." He had to hold on to the fraying thread of resolve.

"I've changed my mind about penetration."

"My beautiful Willow. You're not in any condition to give consent right now."

She sighed out her vexation. And his demanding cock was strangled in his slacks.

Jax held her for a long time, until her breathing returned to normal. Then he helped her to dress.

She grabbed hold of his forearm for support as she slipped into her shoes.

"Give me a minute to clean up the room."

"Isn't the sub supposed to do that?"

"Yeah. But princesses don't."

She gave him a half smile. Was it his imagination, or did the room get brighter? After wiping down the bench, he packed his bag before asking, "Where are you staying?"

"Nearby." She adjusted her skirt. She was back in control and obviously stinging from his denial. "It's close enough to walk. I'll see myself back. Thank you for a nice evening."

"Don't you fucking dare."

"Look—"

"You're not dismissing me, Willow." He was pissed. "I will see you safely back to your hotel."

"You made it clear that we were done." She pulled back her hair and twisted it into some kind of knot.

"Not even for a second. I was honoring your boundaries. And if you have an emotional crash, I'm going to be there. You're not getting rid of me yet, so you might as well quit trying. Your call. You can walk out of here or I can toss you over my shoulder."

She looked at him, studied his stance as if trying to determine how serious he was. Finally, she exhaled a slight huff. "You can secure a ride for me."

"Do I look like I'm open to a compromise?" When she opened her mouth again, his temper unraveled. "Don't make me gag you."

"You—"

"Last chance. I'll give you the world, but I won't risk your safety. Deal with it." He picked up his bag. Then, aware that he might have overreacted because she mattered to him, and not just because she was his investor's kid, he added, "It's a ride." Deep inside, he knew it was so much more for her. Her freedom. Her perceived slight. "Is it worth the argument? Five minutes, Willow."

In the end, she relented with a tight nod.

On the main level, he claimed her lightweight jacket and helped her into it while Trinity called the valet to bring his car around.

Jax took Willow's elbow as they walked down the steep set of stairs leading to the street.

Outside in the warm spring evening, people were everywhere—on the sidewalks, leaning over balconies, weaving through stopped, honking cars on the street. Revelers, some draped in Mardi Gras beads, bustled by, sipping hurricanes.

He guided her toward their waiting car and helped her inside.

When he was in the driver's seat, he asked, "Are you at a hotel or private residence?"

"The Maison Sterling."

"Excellent choice." The boutique hotel known for its exquisite service and accommodations was owned by the Sterling family—fellow Titans.

As she'd said, the hotel was nearby, but with the partiers and gridlock of cars, it might have been faster to walk. Still, they reached their destination sooner than he would have liked. He didn't want their evening to end with her feeling abandoned.

He found a rare parking spot on the street and pulled into it so they had a few more minutes together. "May I buy you a drink?"

"I have an early flight." She shot him a polite smile that was gobbled by the nighttime shadows. "Thanks for the offer. It's nice of you."

There was that infuriating word again, wielded like a weapon.

"I—"

"Come on, Willow!" He slammed his hand on the steering wheel. "As your Dom, as a man, it's my responsibility to take care of you. If I had fucked you as hard as I wanted in that room, I'd be the asshole you think I am."

She leaned back against the headrest.

"I'm trying to be a decent human being."

With a small grin she turned to look at him. The car was intimate and quiet. "Is it as difficult as it sounds?"

"Keeping my hands off you? Yeah. I've got it for you. Bad." He gave into the temptation that was Willow Henderson and leaned across the car to capture her chin. "May I kiss you?"

For a second, she said nothing.

"You've got your chance to reject me." And maybe she should.

"Kiss me, Jax."

He did. At first, he teased, waiting for her response. When she gave it, he slid his hand inside her jacket, then her crop top.

Some idiot kid knocked on the window and gave him a thumbs-up.

Jax shook his head. "I'm going to need more privacy to seduce you."

"Is that what you're doing?"

"If you'll have me."

There was silence. Loud and echoing.

Finally, her words the barest of whispers, she said, "I accept your invitation to join you for a drink."

Pride and possession thrummed through him.

Within minutes, they were in the lobby, and the concierge directed them to an intimate bar. It had old-world elegance, with oversize leather chairs, small round tables, and silver dishes filled with premium nuts. In the center of the room, a musician played a piano, providing a soothing background.

Willow ordered a dry white wine, and he opted for a premium whiskey.

"So…" She regarded him over the rim of her glass. "About this seduction."

"I don't sleep around, and I don't discard women. If we sleep together, there's no going back."

"You really are a knight in shining armor."

"No. A kid with a hard background who tries to do the right thing."

They spent an hour over their drinks. She told him about her studies and shared that she was considering career options for after graduation.

"You can come work for me. Maybe have a positive influence on the office. And me."

She rolled her eyes as if that was impossible. "One could hope."

He tossed out the idea as a way to keep her close—a natural transition—but the more he thought about it, the more sense it made. She saw the world differently than he did. He was smart enough to know that could be a valuable asset. Not many people had the courage to look him in the eye and call him out. "I offer fringe benefits. All the spankings you need."

An interested gleam lightened her eyes, making them appear golden. He adored her many expressions and wanted to explore them all. "Ah, impact play is the key to your kingdom, isn't it? You could come to me anytime and I'd kick anyone else out and lock the door. From time to time, I'd even get you off."

Her breath caught. "That took me by surprise. I don't usually orgasm during a scene." She clapped a hand over her mouth. "Wait! I shouldn't have admitted that. Now you'll be even more insufferable."

"Surely that's impossible."

"You read my mind, Jax."

They shared a grin. Solidarity. He'd take that as a win. "What is it specifically about impact play that satisfies you?"

After laughing, she answered his question sincerely. "I've always channeled my energy into something—ballet, cycling, yoga. But a group of us visited the Quarter a couple of years ago on one of their explore days. There were lots of workshops and discussions, and we had the opportunity to try things, in a very vanilla type of way—over our clothes, that sort of thing. I found peace I hadn't known I was looking for." She took the final sip from her glass. "A spanking refocuses me, chases away stress. I can study better. Sleep better. I don't have to have it all the time. Sometimes just knowing it will happen helps."

"And the men you play with?" His voice was far sharper than he'd intended.

"I've scened with the same top a couple of times. But mostly, I see who's available."

He didn't like that risk.

"Thanks to Aviana, the Quarter is a safe place for me to visit." She slid her empty glass onto the table. "I'm ready for bed."

"Is that an invitation or a dismissal?"

"Despite what you might have believed, I was in total control of my thoughts back at the club when I asked you to make love to me."

He signaled for the check and paid the bill.

They rode the elevator to the third floor. Then, when they were in the room, she hung out the DO NOT DISTURB sign.

This time, he closed the distance with deliberate intent. He loosened the belt of her coat and slid the garment from her shoulders. Then he kissed her the way he wanted to, coaxing a response and then deepening his probing until her mouth was wide and she leaned into him.

When he ended the kiss, she was breathless, and his hunger for her demanded satiation.

In a few calculated moves, he had her undressed. He toed off his boots and spent a few impatient seconds getting rid of his socks before she reached for his belt.

He allowed her to fumble with it long enough for her to sigh in frustration. "Allow me." He managed to get it apart while she unbuttoned his trousers and lowered his zipper.

"You don't wear underwear?" she asked as his trousers fell.

"Another of my many charms."

She struggled with his T-shirt, and his patience reached its end. Lovemaking would have to wait for later. This was about staking his claim.

He captured her under her ass and lifted her from the floor. Obediently she wrapped her legs around his waist, holding on as he carried her to the bed.

She let go and landed on the mattress with a squeal, still reaching for him. Helping her out, he tugged the shirt over his head and dropped it.

"Jax..."

He yanked off her thong and covered her hot pussy with his mouth. She arched, crying his name. He tongued her clit until her words ran together in nonsensical pleasure. "Come for me, princess."

"I want you." She grabbed his head.

He pressed on that tiny nub and placed his finger inside her, making sure she was wet.

"Please..."

He left her long enough to grab a condom from his wallet, and when he returned, he kissed her hard, loving the taste of her on his tongue. She was the sexiest woman he'd ever known.

Willow spread her legs. His dick was already raging, and he didn't need a second invitation. He grabbed her hands and pinned her wrists over her head. "Look at me. I want to see what I do to you." He pressed his cockhead to her entrance.

Her eyes widened. "This is what I want."

Him as well. He stroked in, a little at a time, until he felt some resistance.

"I want you all the way inside me." She pulled free from his grip so she could wrap her arms around his neck. Then she lifted her hips.

He drove deep, then knew the truth. "Holy *fuck*."

"Jax, please."

He pushed up onto his hands to look into her eyes. "You're a *virgin*?"

"After the spanking, the orgasms...I wanted it to be you."

Emotions spiraled through him. Shock. Disbelief. And then...humility. She'd chosen him. No wonder his refusal had been such a rejection for her.

"Don't be mad."

"Mad is the last thing I am." He kissed her again with tenderness.

Now that he knew, now that she'd chosen him, he changed his pace, making love to her rather than fucking her. There'd be time for that later. He stroked in and out, reaching between them to toy with her clit. Then because he knew she liked sensation play, he pinched it, sending her over the edge with a scream.

After he'd satisfied her, he orgasmed.

For long moments, he remained propped up so he could study her, the wonder in her eyes, the satisfied smile on her kissable lips.

When his arms started to shake, he rolled to his side to gather her close, facing him. He stroked her hair, then her spine. Until her, he hadn't known this was missing in his life.

"That was—"

"If you say nice, I'll blister your ass."

"It was…" She smiled lazily. "Everything I dreamed my first time would be."

He sucked in a breath. In his entire life, Jax had never heard sweeter words, ones that meant more. They didn't feed his ego…they opened his heart. Willow had given him the greatest gift imaginable, and he vowed to cherish it. *Her.*

It would take a lifetime to get enough of this, of her. And a lifetime was the perfect solution to the problems he'd caused when he'd scened with her instead of taking her home from the club. Her being a virgin made the next decision as easy as it was inevitable. "We'll get married within a month."

CHAPTER FIVE

Willow shoved him away and struggled out of the viselike strength of his arms. Frantic, she scooted away and sat up. She pulled her knees against her and wrapped her arms around them, as if it would afford some sort of protection against the formidable man in her bed. "You've lost your mind."

He sat up as well, but fortunately allowed her to keep the distance between them. "It's the perfect solution."

"No. It's not. No, no, no, no, no, no, *no*. And in case that's not clear, no." She wasn't ready. Her entire future—away from Houston—pursuing her dreams was waiting. She couldn't allow anyone to derail her. "I'm not marrying anyone. Especially you."

His nostrils flared, and she trembled, knowing she'd well and truly pissed him off.

The world closed in on her. By going to bed with him, she'd been ensnared by the steel trap that was Jaxon Mills.

He reached for her wrist, and claustrophobia closed around her, triggering a need to run. She leaped from the bed so hard that her knees wobbled when she touched the floor.

"Damn it, Willow. Listen to me." He raked a hand down his face, man and fury, naked, his cock hard, and all his muscles and sinews coiled tight, ready to spring.

"Stay where you are!" She raised a hand. "I mean it. I need some space." Her heart thundered so loudly in her ears that it drowned out all other sounds. She hurried across the room to snatch up the thick robe provided by the hotel. With shaking fingers, she knotted the belt.

She backed up against a wall. To his credit, he stayed where he was, even though his jaw was set in implacable lines and temper burned in his eyes. She shuddered.

"Please, come here so we can talk." He'd dropped his tone, removing the threat and making the words an invitation.

"No." Willow refused to be swayed by his skilled vocal inflections. "It's time for you to leave."

"I'm not sure I was clear," he countered, words still measured, not betraying the emotion that was conveyed by the rapid tic in his temples. "We're getting married, Willow. We'll need to work out the details."

Was he deaf? She glared at him as she shook her head. "This isn't the eighteen hundreds, Jax." Hysteria bubbled through her, making it impossible to breathe. "You don't have to protect my virtue."

"Of course I do. I scened with you at the club, then took your virginity."

"Stop it. Please. You didn't take it. I gave it. There's a huge difference." Why had she slept with him? Any other man would have been happy to fuck her and leave her. "I make my own decisions."

He shrugged. "I warned you before I took you to a private room."

"I don't want to get married." Especially to an overbearing alpha male. No matter how sexy.

His fist was clenched, visible proof of the effort it took for him to stay where he was. "I've heard all about you. What about me?"

Him? She barely contained her shock. He was destroying her life and was concerned about himself? "This isn't about you."

"Yeah. It is. I won't get over you, Willow."

Knocked in the solar plexus, she gasped.

"Give me ten minutes," he asked. "Then, if you want, I'll leave without another word."

Willow knew what was good for her. And that meant she shouldn't be in the same room as him. He was far too tempting, and she responded to him on an elemental level—a survival of the species urge. Every part of her wanted him.

His admission that he wouldn't get over her rooted her in place.

"I'm honored you chose me, Willow."

"It was just sex."

"One more crack like that, and I won't be able to keep my hands off you. I'll prove how damn wrong you are."

She tried to take another step back, but she couldn't. Instead, she put a hand on her heart, as if she could protect it.

"But you already know that, don't you?" His words were a whisper, a challenge. He saw her lies and took a scalpel to them.

"Jax…"

"Fucking admit it, princess. You like my kisses, the way you got lost when we scened. And you were alive in a way you've never been when my cock was inside you."

She forced herself to focus on his face and not his honed abs, the hand that had held her in place over his lap as he spanked her, his damnable cock. The problem with that was his lips. She wanted them on her. He might be irresistible, but that didn't mean they should spend the rest of their lives together.

Marriage wasn't in her immediate future. She needed to finish her last semester at school, then establish her career, maybe buy a condominium or a house. When—if—she accepted a proposal, it would be from a man she'd spent a lot of time with and knew well. They'd have similar interests and shared vision for the future. She was looking for a deep, abiding love, such as her parents had. Their years of infertility and miscarriages hadn't driven them apart. Instead, the struggle had bound them more closely together. They supported each other through the tough times, and they celebrated each joy along the way. They'd dated for years before marrying. "All right," she conceded. "We have insta-lust. Which you seem to equate with some sort of misplaced sense of obligation." If she'd had any idea he would stake a claim on some moral high ground, she would have locked her virginity up in a chastity belt.

"It's more than some fleeting attraction that's going to be satisfied by us going at it a couple of times. And there's no misplaced anything. Admit it."

Her legs lost strength, so she moved to an armchair to sit down.

"I'm a possibility thinker, Willow. And I see the start of something good here. We could make a good team. An excellent one, even. You have talents that Jaxon Media needs and that I value."

"You're not listening to me."

"I have eight minutes left."

It seemed to have escaped him that she actually hadn't agreed to his request. He was a relentless force of nature.

"This is opportunity for both of us."

"Is that what I am to you?" Her skin prickled. "An *opportunity*?"

"I meant no offense." He held up an apologetic hand. "With your degree in social work, you'll have a perspective of the world that I don't. You think money is being squandered or at the least could be put to better use. You would have my full support in your endeavors. Perhaps you could establish a foundation and you could be in charge of it, or at least the final decision maker. As you may have noticed, I have an already-established platform you can use."

At what cost? Putting up with him every day? Enduring his attitude?

"Every relationship starts somewhere. Successful couples have a shared vision. I'd like to support some sort of charity for kids, camps, that sort of thing. That's something we can work on together."

Damn him. Jaxon Mills, master persuader, had captured her interest.

"Tell me you'll think about it."

She didn't want to. But she was already picturing herself happily giving away his fortune.

"You're someone who will stand up to me, tell me when I'm wrong, help me be a better person. Love will come, Willow. If we nurture it and allow it."

She let out a shaky breath. He was so very tempting.

"We need to get to know each other. I understand that. So tell me what you want in a husband?"

"I'm *not* looking for a husband," she reminded him.

"Okay, we'll do it your way. Hypothetically."

She didn't want to soften toward him, but he was wicked good at changing her mood. "Things in common."

"We both like sex."

A tingle shot up her spine at the way he narrowed his eyes. "Sex isn't a good basis for a relationship."

"Okay. Agreed. So tell me what is."

Willow needed to stop this conversation before it went any further. "I know what you're doing, Jax."

"What's that?"

"You're hoping I'll convince myself that marrying you is a good idea."

"Caught me." He grinned. "You are wise to my nefarious ways."

Damn him for being irresistible.

"Indulge me. What else matters to you in a life mate?"

She might be wise to his nefarious ways, but she wasn't immune to them. "Common values."

"And we both agreed, no cheating."

"Is everything about sex with you?"

"At this moment. Where you're concerned, yes." His dick pointed straight up.

"That wasn't what I meant. I meant like family, children. How we spend our time." Once again on solid ground, she folded her arms.

"I want kids. And we both plan to do good on the planet."

She scowled. "By using a carrot instead of a stick."

"I'm open to discussion," he conceded.

He was? "You are?"

"We would make a good team. What other attributes in Mr. Hypothetical?"

This time, when he left the bed, she didn't stop him. He walked toward her, a step at a time.

"Love. I want to be loved."

"I'd say we've got potential." With extreme gentleness, he held her by the waist. "The idea of another man touching you enrages me. This isn't any fancy social-worker term, Willow. It's raw. It's real." He stroked her hipbones with his thumbs. "I'm exposing my heart knowing I could get hurt badly. It's a risk I've never taken with anyone else."

"You've swept me up in some sort of storm."

"I'll keep you safe from them." He leaned toward her, his eyes vibrant, intent on her. Now she knew how he'd built his empire. When he focused on something, he was relentless in its pursuit. Yet his words weren't grandiose—they were filled with sincerity.

Maybe he wasn't all bad. *Maybe.*

"I'd like to kiss you."

A sensation rocked her, that of standing on the edge of a cliff and wanting to jump. "If you do, it doesn't mean we have to get married."

"Of course not."

She looked at his face, trying to decipher his words. "I'm not sure I believe you."

"Oh Willow. Do you ever give up?"

"Do you?" she countered.

"See there? And you thought we had nothing in common." He smiled, draining away her tension. "Now, as for that kiss."

"Yes." She cradled his face and rose on her tiptoes to meet him.

Jax wrapped his arms around her and claimed her mouth with tenderness and a heartfelt promise.

Once he recognized her surrender, he deepened the kiss, his tongue plundering her, asking for more than he'd taken before.

Lost, she clung to him and gave him what he demanded.

He groaned from deep inside, and his cock pressed into her. Boldly, she reached between them to cup his balls, then stroke his shaft. Jax broke off the kiss and pulled back to grab her hand and force her to stop. "God, no, princess. I don't have another condom in my wallet."

"I could just do this." She'd never jacked off a man before, but with the way his body went rigid, she guessed she was doing something he liked.

"No. I mean, yes. You're amazing, but I want to be inside you." He moved her hand away from his cock. "I need to make a trip to the gift shop. I promise you, we can make love all night. Or at least until I have to put you on a plane in the morning."

Her earlier white lie chafed. Before she could admit the truth, he said, "Condoms. Now. You want to come downstairs with me?"

"I actually haven't eaten. So yes."

"I'll take you somewhere. What would you like to go?"

"Downstairs. Every night at ten, they have a pizza party in the lobby."

"Pizza?" Disdain dripped from the word, making her laugh.

"All kinds of different choices, and they have several different craft beers that they sample. It's the main reason I stay here."

"It's New Orleans. Some of the best steak and seafood places in the country are within walking distance. There's a place on Chartres Street that serves Cajun food. Their sampler plate is divine. Gumbo, étouffée, red beans and rice, and jambalaya. If you need bread, I know a place with a great shrimp po'boy."

"You don't have to eat pizza. Just don't judge my choice."

He sighed. "You win."

"How sweet that sounds."

He flicked a glance toward her discarded outfit. "Do you have other clothes?"

"Yes, Jax. I brought more than BDSM wear with me."

"Good thing, or you wouldn't be leaving this room."

She sighed. Not as self-conscious as she thought she'd be, she dropped the robe, then walked to the dresser to pull out a bra and fresh panties before selecting a pair of jeans and a T-shirt with a motivational saying on it. *Positive vibes. Positive life.* Then she grabbed one of her dad's old dress shirts. After slipping into it, she tied the tails into a knot at her waist. Finally, she added a pair of comfortable sandals. With her mussed hair and ruined makeup, she was no femme fatale.

Willow sank onto the edge of the mattress and watched Jax pull on his boots.

She'd lived with Lawrence for almost a month, and she'd been on guard the entire time, dressing in the closet, never emerging from the bathroom without something covering her. It wasn't until now that she realized she'd never trusted him.

Which meant... She inhaled. Even if he annoyed the crap out of her, Jax was an honorable man.

He glanced up to catch her staring at him. "Everything okay?"

Except for the way she ached to touch him, run her fingers across his face, reveling in the friction of his scruff as he leaned toward her to claim a casual, quick kiss that she associated with couples who'd been in a long-term relationship. "Lost in thought."

Still keeping an eye on her, he stood and buckled his belt. "Tell me they at least have a Margherita pizza."

"I've never looked, but they have so many different options, it's hard to imagine they wouldn't have it."

After ensuring they had a room key, they walked to the elevator.

It wasn't until the doors slid open that she realized that he'd distracted her with a kiss earlier instead of agreeing that they didn't have to get married.

Since there were other guests in the car, she wasn't able to ask him about it.

When they reached the lobby, it was to find dozens of people milling around.

"Quite the spread," he observed.

"Isn't it the best?" There were two tables to choose from. The first had pizzas and garlic knots. The second had desserts, all made from the same delicious dough but crafted with the hotel's special flair. There were cinnamon rolls, an apple pie, even melted chocolate stuffed between two crusts.

This party was definitely her style, even if it wasn't his. With his abs and tight ass, he no doubt deprived himself of all happiness-giving carbs and exercised like a fiend. Not that she minded.

"Next dinner has to be at a proper restaurant."

"But tonight?" She raised her eyebrows. "Tonight we enjoy a gastronomic feast!" She grabbed his hand and dragged him toward the first table where she shoved a plate and several napkins into his hand before selecting two ridiculously large pieces for herself.

He looked around. "Do they have salad?"

"Oh my God. Seriously?" She rolled her eyes. "Stop. They have a veggie pizza over there. And I see the Margherita one as well." She pointed to the far end of the table. "And there's beer, of course."

"Excuse me?"

"Hops. Barley. They grow from the ground, right? Hence, beer is salad."

"Is my future going to be filled with this kind of logic?"

"Hopefully not. You could have a magnificent change of heart and forget you ever saw me."

"Not a chance."

She sighed. "Please, not another word." She'd been right earlier when she said he never gave up. "You don't get to ruin my pizza party." Since there were others in line who wanted the food as much as she did, she walked away from the table. "Want a beer?"

He joined her at the bar where the server described the evening's three options and ending with his suggestions. "The lager pairs nicely with the Margherita pizza, complementing the charred crust and sweetness of the sauce," he said. "Perfect for you, sir." He poured a small sample. "Ma'am, may I recommend the brown ale? It will help deliver a complex finish to your meal." He poured a second taster.

"Who knew pizza and beer could be so complicated?" Jax asked.

In the end, he went with the lager, and she selected the brown ale. They found a couple of bistro chairs around a wrought-iron table and settled in.

She took the first savory bite and closed her eyes in pleasure. When she finally reached for a drink of her beer, he was staring at her.

"I could watch you eat all night long. You're all smiles and sighs."

"Pizza is my favorite. I buy one every Sunday and eat it for dinner every night of the week. So I never have to cook dinner." Midway through the second piece, she gave up.

"That was quite impressive."

Hating to admit defeat, she eyed it. "If pepperoni had been the only topping, I could have finished it."

A server took their plates, and they carried the remainder of their drinks to a comfortable couch in a secluded corner. The lighting was soft, and the area was quiet.

She kicked off her sandals and curled up near him, holding her beer. "You mentioned a children's charity, such as supporting a camp. A summer school type of thing? Or after school?"

"So you are intrigued?"

"Of course. I think having places for kids to go, something to do is essential. Even community centers—free ones—are wonderful. Anywhere with adult supervision. Interaction."

"Not everyone is fortunate enough to have resources when they're growing up."

There was something different in his tone. An underlying pain she'd never suspected.

"You've never listened to my videos, have you?"

Pretending she'd been uncomfortable, she shifted her weight, tucking her legs the opposite direction.

"Otherwise you'd know my story. I left home at fifteen with cracked ribs and a black eye."

Shock rendered her silent.

"My dad did it."

"Your mom didn't stop him?"

Jax's words were emotionless, but his eyes were turbulent. "I tell my story often as inspiration, but I rarely talk about my mom, so this part is personal and not to be shared."

When she nodded, he went on. "She left when I was young." He shrugged. "I'm not sure how old I was. The memories are fuzzy." He took a long drink of his beer before sliding it onto a nearby table. "I don't know her name. Only thing I ever heard my dad call her was bitch. Whore. And a couple more colorful descriptions."

"Oh Jax. I had no idea." His struggle made his success all the more remarkable.

"He always suspected I wasn't his, but I suppose we'll never know. She swore I was legitimate, but one night when he was drunk, he called me a bastard, and not in the asshole way."

She waited for him to go on.

"A teacher took pity on me and nominated me for a scholarship to summer camp one year, and my dad let me go because they fed me breakfast and lunch and that was less money he had to shell out for my miserable existence. His words."

Her hand shook.

"I learned about acting and creating video."

"Your first five dollars." She gave a half smile. "Five. Your lucky number."

He took his wallet from his back pocket and pulled out the bill. It was worn with time and handling, and it looked different from the currency she'd recently seen in circulation.

"My dad found other money hidden in my room. That's why he snapped. I made my own way. Stayed with friends, slept on couches. Somehow managed to get a GED even though I dropped out of school at sixteen."

How could she not want to help him support other kids? He was dragging her into his web. She had to be careful not to capitulate entirely.

Her phone vibrated in her back pocket. "My mother, I'm sure."

"Go ahead." He took a drink of beer while he watched her.

She typed in a reply and a heart emoji before putting the phone upside down on the table. "She often sends news from home. It's her way of checking on me."

"Your parents care about you."

"The spoiled, pampered child." She sighed. "That's what you think, right? What a lot of people believe." And one of the reasons she'd refused to let her mom and dad pay for grad school.

"There's a deeper side to you."

"I'm the child they never thought they could have. I'm sure you don't know that they tried to have a baby for a lot of years, and Mom suffered a number of miscarriages."

"All their hopes and dreams are on your shoulders."

"Sounds petty, compared to your background."

"No need to compare. Family dynamics are often complicated, as you know."

"They are. No matter how well-meaning. They are more than protective. Mom used to call my college to make sure I was okay. I can't imagine what she would do if I didn't come home for breaks." She took another sip of the brew, this time for fortification. "If they find out that I'm here…"

"Not a matter of if."

"You're hell-bent on giving my mother a nervous breakdown?"

He grinned. "Not swayed. I think Andrea is made of sterner stuff."

"Not when it comes to me." Andrea had devoted the past twenty-two years to motherhood, and the bonds wouldn't be broken lightly.

"Then she'll be glad if you return to Houston."

"Jaxon?"

A man strode toward them, hand extended. Jaxon stood to greet him. "Rykker."

She watched the two, about the same height, shake hands. It was impossible to miss the display of strength and masculine prowess. Sometimes she wondered how far alpha males had progressed since the caveman days.

"Have you met Willow Henderson?"

Rykker turned toward her with a polite smile. "Brian and Andrea's daughter?"

Her incognito trip was now well and truly ruined. Glowering at Jax, she stood, trying to stuff her feet back into her discarded sandals. "Nice to meet you." The words were polite, nothing more.

She accepted his offered hand, and he was gentle with her.

"My fiancée," Jax added.

Her smile froze.

"Congratulations." Rykker smiled, and she extracted her hand. "When's the big day?"

"Soon."

She called on the etiquette classes her mother had forced her to attend in order not to choke Jax and step over his dead body.

"Willow," he went on, either oblivious or not giving a damn, "Rykker King. He chairs the Zetas membership committee, and he has a hand in a number of our philanthropic ventures. Fair warning, Rykker, my future bride thinks we should be doing much more than we are."

"Is that correct?" He met her gaze with interest, forcing her to maintain her society smile. "Feel free to reach out to me. Now, if you'll excuse, me, I'm meeting Judge Anderson for a drink."

"Give Gideon my regards."

"I will." He gave her a slight bow. "Nice to meet you, Ms. Henderson."

She remained where she was until he was out of earshot. "That was an underhanded move, Jax. And I don't appreciate it."

"Better he would think we're having a tryst?"

She clenched her hands at her sides.

"I need to get you to bed. How early is your flight?"

Her thoughts screeched to a stop. "Uhm…"

He folded his arms and waited.

She flicked a frantic glance toward his right hand, remembering the way he'd scorched her buttocks.

"Willow?"

"It's on Sunday."

"You lied to me?" His voice dropped an octave and took her stomach with it.

"A little one. Tiny. Itty-bitty. You know, a polite one."

"You may want to stop right there."

"It was harmless. Something people say to avoid hurting feelings."

"Lying to me is never harmless."

She shuddered. "Neither is telling people we're getting married."

"We should go upstairs. And we'll need condoms."

Fortunately there were only a few choices, unlike the displays she'd seen at the local drugstore. She pretended to look at a magazine while he made his selection. *Extra – large of course.*

After paying, he slid the box into his front pocket before capturing her elbow and guiding her toward the valet stand. "I have a bag in my car. Can you have someone get it for me?" He slid a twenty-dollar bill onto the counter.

"Right away, sir."

He gave the room number and information on his car. "Oh, and a bucket of ice."

Heat rushed through her, as if the man knew what Jax intended.

With a wicked grin, he said, "Ready?"

During the ride up, she cast furtive glances his way, but he focused on the button for each floor as it lit up.

"It was before we had sex, you know. The fib, I mean. A polite way to end the evening."

He didn't respond.

"Uhm, how about if I promise never to do that again?"

"I'd appreciate that." He looked at her. "I will never lie to you. The truth stings once, and it can be damn brutal. Lies sting with every memory. So I promise you, I will be honest with you. Even if you don't like it."

She nodded. "And in return, the nature of our relationship is private from the outside world."

"I was protecting your reputation."

Willow almost argued. Almost. But he was alpha enough, stubborn enough, to spend the rest of the night insisting there was a difference.

As soon they were in the room, he had her against the door. "I don't want anyone looking at you."

How much was about her reputation, and how much was about him staking a claim? His eyes were intent, and he placed a gentle kiss on her forehead. All of her concerns vanished.

He stroked the side of her breast, and desire slammed into her. "Yes," she whispered.

Jax lifted her from the floor, and she wrapped her legs around his waist and grabbed hold of his shoulders.

His eyes were predatory.

"I'm not scared of you." Because she knew he had her, she fed her fingers into his thick hair.

"You need to touch me more often." He claimed her mouth, tasting of possession.

Willow dragged in the scent of him, that of sex and confidence. She ached for him.

Somehow, he managed to get her to the bed, but before he could unknot her shirttails, a loud knock on the door interrupted them. "Better now than later?" she asked.

"For damn sure."

He tipped the bellman and wished the man a good night.

Once the PRIVACY PLEASE sign was hanging from the knob, Jax closed the door. He slid the ice bucket onto the nightstand, then placed the toy bag on top of her suitcase. "Since you're here for another day, I've decided to extend my stay. We can explore the city, go back to Quarter if you wish. Get some decent food." He pulled out the box of condoms, opened it, and dumped out the three packages. "Maybe I should have bought a second box."

He tossed one of the condoms on the mattress. "This time, I want to undress you." He pointed to a spot on the floor right in front of him. "Come here, Willow."

CHAPTER SIX

Everything about Willow turned him on. He loosened the knot she'd tied in the shirttails and then pushed back the shirt from her shoulders. Then he had the chance to read her T-shirt. "Motivational phrases on your clothing?"

"Well, a couple are about mimosas and happy hour. I have one about pizza."

He grinned. Of course. "No offense. I like you better out of your clothes." He reached behind her to unfasten her bra. Her nipples were gloriously hard, and he couldn't resist the urge to caress her.

She hissed in a breath.

"Too much?"

"No. Not enough."

"You're mine, princess." He left her long enough to grab a piece of ice. "Your introduction to sensation play." He sucked the cube into his mouth to melt it a little. "Offer yourself to me."

After a slight hesitation, she cupped her breasts.

"Since all of this is an exploration, you can safe word or use *yellow*. We'll learn more about each other as we go forward."

She nodded.

He touched the frozen water to her right nipple, and she sucked in a little breath. The temperature was obviously a shock, but the moment he moved on, she shimmied. "How was that?"

"I liked it."

"Yeah. Me too." He repeated his action on her left breast. Her flesh contracted, then swelled, begging for more. He could spend forever exploring her.

When she was covered in goose bumps, moaning and rocking toward him, he tossed the cube back into the bucket. "I'd say your first experience with temperature play is a win."

"Yes." She was clenching her buttocks, as if fighting arousal.

He appreciated the way she'd been willing to try the ice. Even more, he enjoyed her reaction. "I want you out of your pants."

She kicked off her sandals while he unfastened the snap at her waistband and lowered the short zipper.

He dropped to his knees after he'd stripped off her jeans and lacy panties.

Then he selected another piece of ice. "Hands behind your back, princess. And if you lose balance, you can grab my shoulders, but you can't attempt to push me away."

Gaze riveted on his hand, she nodded and did as he said. He tongued her pussy, and she moaned in surrender. His caveman instinct flared, and he renewed his internal vow to have her down the aisle and his ring on her finger within the week.

She grabbed him for support. "Cold and heat… God. Yes. I can't think."

He tossed the remaining ice chip into the bucket. Her pussy was red, and he inhaled the intoxicating musk of her arousal.

He pushed to his feet and backed her onto the bed. He hurriedly dropped his clothes, not caring where they landed. "Condom."

Willow searched around for it and finally offered it to him.

"You do it," he instructed.

"I've never done it before."

The first touch of her hand on his dick almost made him shoot off. "Stop. On second thought, that's not a good idea." His words were gruffer than he intended.

It took him much longer to get the damn thing on than it ever had before. Before sliding into her, he took a breath to put himself back in control.

With slow, gentle motions, he moved inside her.

"Jax, faster," she urged. "That ice...your mouth."

"I want to be sure your pussy isn't too tender."

"I'm fine," she insisted, eyes flashing, digging her hands into his hair to pull him toward her.

Her urgency rocked him, and he wanted to give her more power. "Why don't we try something different?"

"Now?"

"You'll like it." Since she was so much smaller and lighter, he was able to reverse their positions with minimal effort, and within seconds she was astride him.

"Really?"

"Yeah. This way you can set the pace." He fisted his cock and held it while she lowered herself toward him.

"I feel awkward."

"We'll do it together."

She winced slightly as his cock entered her.

"Damn it, Willow. You are sore."

"I'm fine." She rocked her hips. "Oh. It's —"

"Watch your choice of words," he teased.

"Awesome?"

"That will work."

It took a few strokes for her to find a position and rhythm that she liked, and then she began to move faster. He curved his hands around her hips, helping her balance.

She closed her eyes and tipped her head. Her hair spilled around her shoulders in a magnificent riot of blonde and fire. He was captivated. "You're exquisite."

"So much deeper this way."

"Yeah."

She rode him, her breaths shortening the faster she moved. "Jax!"

"Come for me, princess."

Her pussy tightened around him. He concentrated on her, watching her climax, and he ground his back teeth to stave off his own orgasm.

Finally, with a sexy whimper, she collapsed onto his chest. He wrapped his arms around her, cherishing her.

A minute or so later, she put her palms on his chest and lifted her head a little. "I had no idea."

"It'll get better, too."

"I'm not sure how it could."

He grinned and chose not to point out that she'd fed his ego.

"But, uhm, you didn't, I mean…"

"Come? No. I can live without it."

"No. Let's… I mean…" A hint of scarlet stained her cheeks.

He'd never been more charmed. "Here." Jax helped her off him before he started stroking his cock. She turned on her side to watch, and her scrutiny was so damn sexy. "Want to do it?" he asked. When she nodded, he removed his hand and allowed her to take over.

"This is nice, but I'd like you inside me."

"Say no more."

She wriggled onto her back, and he rolled on top of her. He slid a finger inside her pussy to arouse her again before easing in. His fierce virgin with the kind heart was his undoing.

Willow moved with him, unselfconscious of her sighs of pleasure. In a scene or in bed, she was freer than she was anywhere else. Her pussy clenched, and he wondered if she would come again.

He readjusted himself to press a finger against her clit and she jerked, crying out a climax. No doubt the ice had made her nerve endings more sensitive. Which was all the reason he needed to keep a supply close at hand.

Consumed with her, he gave in to his own orgasm. It rocketed through him, more powerful than the one before. The more they knew each other, the deeper their connection grew.

He traced her nose. "I meant it earlier. The gift of your virginity...the way you respond to me. I would never get over you."

For a few minutes, he held her before realizing a warm bath would probably do her a world of good.

It took some time to convince her it was okay for them to share the bathroom. Once she sank into the tub of steaming water and closed her eyes, she no longer seemed to care that he entered the shower.

"You were right," she said, watching him while he dried off. "I needed this."

She stayed in there long enough that she needed to top off the hot water. The mirror had steamed over before she reluctantly accepted his hand to help her out of the tub.

He dried her off, then took her to bed, naked.

"This feels naughty. And I might freeze."

"I'll keep you warm," he promised.

She rested her head on his biceps and he snuggled her close and drew up a sheet.

"I've never done this."

"Slept with a man? Slept in the nude?"

Willow was quiet for so long he wasn't sure she was going to answer. "You're the only man I've ever been naked with." She took a breath. "I lived with a guy for a little while, but... Something wasn't right."

He stiffened.

"Feminine intuition, I don't know. Friends set us up, and we got along well. At first, we went out as a group, and then we became exclusive. After about six months, he invited me to move in, and he said he was okay with not having sex. It wasn't that I had something against it. I just wanted to be sure. I saw a bunch of my friends fall in love, and it was sex that made things messy. Emotionally, I mean. I wasn't sure I wanted to get so tangled up that I couldn't get back out."

Yet she'd slept with him.

"After a week or so, he made a move on me when he'd been drinking, and it pissed me off. Then little things started to add up. He would come home late, with vague excuses that he'd had to work late or had to stay for a meeting."

"He was cheating."

"Yeah. He was annoyed that I wouldn't put out."

"He wasn't good enough for you."

"That's one of the reasons I come to the Quarter, Jax." She sat up to look at him. "I don't date. And I won't go to a club in New York, just in case someone I know is there. It's something I need."

"I'll take you as often as you want." No matter how earnest her pleas were, he wasn't going to relent. "Sex is complicated for me too."

"Men don't have the same feelings about it that women do."

"That's a broad stroke. And not true for me. Because I didn't know my mom, don't know whether I'm legitimate or the bastard my dad thinks I am, I controlled my impulses. I didn't want to hurt any kid of mine the way I'd been hurt."

She steepled her hands in front of her face.

"I channeled all my energy and time into making something of myself and helping others along the way. Maybe you don't like the way I do it, but I kick the asses of a million people a day, men and women who rely on me for their dose of inspiration. So, Willow, I mean it when I say sex is damn important to me. Which is why I cherish the fact you chose me. You were absolutely right to be wary. Sleeping with a man came with a whole lot of consequences for you."

Willow's favorite song blasted through the room, dragging her from her sleep. Who the hell was calling her so early? She glanced over at the phone's screen. *Dad.* Of course. Who else would it be? Obviously after slipping from bed before dawn with a promise to return with drinks, Jax had called her father.

She tossed a pillow on top of the device, trying to shut out its happy, annoying tune.

After three more rings, it fell silent, and she was on edge as she waited for her dad to try again.

Knowing she wouldn't be able to go back to sleep, she propped pillows behind her and sat up. She'd been well and truly sucked into Jaxon's vortex. She didn't regret their scene or offering him her virginity. With him, she had completion that she'd never experienced before. On the other hand, no man had ever irritated her more. Why the hell did he have to be a self-proclaimed knight in shining armor?

The phone rang again. She couldn't dodge her father all day. Her voice tight with fake sincerity, she answered. "Morning, Dad."

"Congratulations, Willow."

She dragged the blanket around her bare breasts. How much did he know? Afraid to unintentionally reveal something, she kept her mouth shut.

"Jaxon asked for permission to marry you. Of course, your mother wishes she had more time..."

What? Her father's voice buzzed in her ears, but she couldn't make out a single word.

"But she finds Jax's suggestion agreeable."

She shook her head. "Wait. Can you repeat that? What suggestion?"

Her dad sighed. "She's agreeable to a private ceremony in the next month or so, but she wants you to have the full church wedding and big reception later. She thinks it will take at least a year to plan it."

The vortex tightened around her.

"I'd put your mother on, but she's busy talking to her friends and searching for venues. She's thinking about the Sterling Downtown. Their rooftop atrium, perhaps? Jax mentioned you don't have time to be involved in many of the decisions because of your studies."

Good of him.

She pulled the covers over her head. She'd been right when she said she was going to end up hating him.

"I'll let you get back to your future husband."

"I haven't agreed yet."

"Oh." Silence echoed. "Well, then. Do keep us posted. Your mother will need as much time as she can get."

After a few more minutes, they hung up.

By the time Jax returned, she was dressed in blue jeans and wearing a T-shirt with an inspirational saying. Despite the fact that she was pacing the confines of the room, she was in control, no longer the woman who'd done scandalous things with the billionaire.

"Morning." He held a cardboard to-go tray containing two cups. "Room service will be up with breakfast in half an hour."

She took a step toward him and pointed a finger at his chest. "My dad called."

"Ah. I expected he would." His lips twitched. "I'm crazy about you, princess."

And...she was lost. His transformation from resolved to shocked to humored unraveled the knot in her stomach. She lowered her hand.

He held the tray between them, either as a peace offering or to ward her off, she wasn't sure which.

"I don't drink coffee."

"It's green tea."

"How did you...?"

"I remembered. That day you visited my office. You brought your own drink with you."

His voice wrapped around her in provocative tendrils. It was so much easier to keep emotional distance from him when she wasn't inhaling his scent. "Don't do nice things when I'm mad."

"Would it be so bad? Being my wife? Knowing I'll take care of you?"

"I don't need a man for that."

"Of course not. I'm not questioning your capability or resolve. You've argued with me more than any other person. All within the first eighteen hours that I spent alone with you."

Despite herself, she considered his question. Would it be so bad? Having her BDSM and sexual desires satisfied? She might not want to go to work for him, but the charity sounded exciting. And she'd always planned to return to Houston at some point.

She accepted the tea and took a long drink. "It's wonderful."

"I like waking up with you." He lifted his cup in a salute. "Here's to many more mornings like this."

He was a whirlwind that she wasn't sure how to hold back. "In case you've forgotten, I haven't agreed to marry you," she warned. "There's no way I'd drop out of school or transfer."

"I'll relocate until you're finished."

"That's not possible." She blinked. "You can't just move your office." The logistics would be a nightmare.

"No one but you has the audacity to tell me what I can and can't do. You'll need to fly home to get the marriage license."

"This is ludicrous."

"Would a spanking help convince you?"

Damn him. It would. And he knew it.

Wordlessly, he took her cup from her and set it safely on the desk. "Do you have a hairbrush?"

Her blood turned sluggish as she began the ascent to the alternate reality where worries slipped away.

"Willow?"

She nodded. "It's in the bathroom."

"Fetch it."

While she complied, she heard him slide the drapes closed. When she returned, he was standing near the foot of the bed with his arms folded. He was forceful and intimidating. Even though her pussy still throbbed from they way he'd fucked her so hard last night, she couldn't wait to be dominated again.

"Remove all your clothes and then place your palms flat on the mattress."

God, his voice. So uncompromising. Exactly what she wanted in the bedroom. Aware of his watchful gaze, she did as he instructed. This was different than last night. He hadn't asked for a striptease, and there were no sexual underpinnings.

"I'll always give you this." It was as if he'd seen into her psyche.

Which made him perfect for her.

He caressed her skin, but he didn't warm her up like he had last night. "I want you to feel it. And if you have a few marks to remember this, I'll be happy."

Willow nodded.

"Spread your legs. Your inner thighs and pussy are not safe from me."

She shivered as she adjusted herself.

"Your safe word will always be respected. Use it at any time."

The first crack of the hairbrush knocked her forward. Everything inside her settled. *Yes.* Unprompted, she added, "Thank you."

He was methodical as he applied the implement to her skin. As promised, he covered her inner thighs, making her sway. Then he caught her pussy with his bare hand. Though he'd been gentle, she whimpered. The scorch of pain receded almost immediately, leaving her more turned her on more than she could have imagined. "That was…" She couldn't complete the sentence.

Jax continued until her arms gave out and she collapsed on the mattress in a pile of sobs. He hadn't taken her to subspace, but he'd made her vibrantly alive.

Suddenly, he tossed the brush aside, then smoothed his palms over her heated flesh. She needed this. *Him.*

With tenderness, he helped her up and turned her to face him. She was still wobbly, so she reached for his shoulders for balance. "Will you make love to me?"

"Princess, I'd do anything for you. Anything."

She tugged his shirt from his waistband, reveling in his honed, sexy abs.

With a ridiculous grin, he lifted his arms so she could finish undressing him. "Are you sure you're up for it?"

Even after her long soak last night, her pussy was sore from the immense size of his cock. But she didn't dare tell him that. Instead, she settled for, "I'll take another bath afterward."

"You can't get enough of me, can you?"

"There should be a way for us to put your ego in a box or something." She dropped his shirt.

Catching her off guard, he captured her wrists and linked them behind her.

His eyes were dark, beseeching. All traces of teasing vanished. "I'm falling in love with you, Willow."

Her pulse surged.

"Tell me you'll marry me." The tremor of doubt in his voice was endearing. This really did matter to him. With his expression and tone, he revealed another part of himself, one vulnerable to being hurt. Her emotions softened.

Still, she hesitated a little. "Maybe it wouldn't be so bad, like you said. But I need some time to get used to the idea.

"More than a month?"

This time, his persistence made her laugh. "Three."

"Done."

What? He'd agreed?

With a gleam in his eyes, he capitalized on her shock by kissing her soundly.

Within moments, she yielded to him and linked her arms around his neck. If he was willing to take a risk, she would, too.

"How would you like to celebrate?" he asked, eyes still as intense, but this time with sexual desire. He backed her up toward the bed. "I have a suggestion or two, if you're interested."

"Oh, Sir. Yes." This was a pretty good beginning to their happily ever after.

EPILOGUE

"You're a beautiful bride."

Jax's intimate words, feathered against her ear, made Willow soar. "The gown is wonderful."

"It is." He pressed his palm on her bare back. "Your mom made an excellent choice."

Her mother had visited a store known as one of the best in town. The owner, Randy, had spent hours with her, looking at dresses. They'd linked Willow in by video, but she'd been so overwhelmed and distracted with school and having Jax living with her that she hadn't been able to decide. So they'd proceeded on their own. The gown flattered her figure and flared out at the bottom. She loved it.

"But it's the woman who makes the dress," Jax finished.

The evening couldn't be more magical. She was in his arms on the dance floor of the rooftop atrium of Houston's Sterling Downtown Hotel. The area had been lit with twinkling lights, and a nearly full moon radiated in the sky above. A jazz quartet serenaded them. Despite the fifty or so people watching from the sidelines, Jax stared at her as if she were the center of the universe.

"How long do we have to stay?"

"The cocktail hour ends in about twenty minutes. Then we need to eat. We'll be expected to share a few dances, have some cake, and then my dad is planning a toast."

"I know what I want to eat."

Scandalized, she blushed. "It was you who decided we shouldn't have sex until after the wedding." No matter what she'd tried, from vamp to vixen, to naughty schoolgirl, he hadn't relented. He'd given her the BDSM scenes she wanted, but he'd insisted they take time to get to know each other, and since she'd said all he thought about was sex, he was determined that they should develop a friendship and give themselves unfettered freedom to fall in love.

During the last few months, he'd been amazing. He'd scaled back his work hours, made sure she ate more than pizza for dinner, and they'd brainstormed the foundation he was going to establish. The more time they spent together, the deeper she fell for him.

He was still brash on his show, shouting that people should drag their asses out of bed an hour earlier to chase their dreams, but he'd tempered it somewhat. Last month, he'd done a show for high school students, and he'd listened more than he'd talked. She'd accepted his challenge and watched the video of him speaking at the high school graduation that he'd mentioned. He was more complex than she'd originally believed. And he'd admitted that being with her was helping him grow.

All that was wonderful, but she was ready to crawl out of her skin from sexual need. Once she'd suggested they elope just so he'd take her to bed.

The dance ended, and a few other couples joined them for a more up-tempo tune.

Shortly after, she and Jax left the floor to mingle. Her father shook Jax's hand, then took her shoulders and met her eyes. "I hope he makes you happy. If he doesn't, I have a shotgun."

Her mother was all smiles as she kissed Willow's cheeks. "I can't wait for your big ceremony! This was so much fun that I'm thinking of becoming a wedding planner."

"You'd be perfect, Mrs. Henderson," Jax said. "I'll do a few promo spots for you and give you some social media pointers."

"No. No, no, no." Willow scowled at him. "I'll give you the pointers, Mom."

He shrugged.

"You have your hands full, my boy," Brian said.

101

"I consider myself lucky." He stroked the length of her spine as he spoke.

Rafe Sterling, owner of the hotel, exited the private elevator and walked over to join them. "I wanted to be among the first to offer my congratulations."

She'd known Rafe for several years, and stress lines were now grooved next to his eyes. Rumor had it that his father had abandoned his family and the business, leaving Rafe to sort out the mess.

"And I wanted to thank you for comping the Honeymoon Suite," Jax replied. "That wasn't necessary."

"It's my pleasure."

"So when are you finally going to come on my show? I stayed at the Maison Sterling recently. Exceptional service," Jax said. "My viewers want to hear your philosophies on hospitality, what you do different, how you consistently win top marks in the industry. They want to hear from winners."

"We'll set something up."

For the remainder of the cocktail hour, they chatted with guests, including Rykker King, whom she'd met in New Orleans.

Later, during dinner, Jax leaned toward her. Against her ear, he said, "Dinner is taking too damn long."

"It was your idea for us to be celibate until tonight." She tried to hide her smile.

"I'm having a fantasy. About fucking you while you're wearing the gown."

Her new husband's words made her blush. The realization that she was his forever made her shiver anew. Every time she looked at him, tingles jumped through her. She wondered if that sensation would ever go away.

"Just pull it up and take you from behind."

She dropped her fork.

From the other side of the table, her mother cast her a concerned glance.

Jax chuckled. "Smile, princess."

She gave her mother a reassuring nod.

Jax stayed by her side the entire evening, and after her father gave his toast, Jax stood.

"I hope it's okay if I say something."

The crowd laughed. No one expected that Jaxon Mills would have resisted the siren's call of an open microphone.

He faced her, as did everyone else in the room.

"In a man's life, if he's lucky, he meets a woman who completes his heart."

Her eyes filled with tears and her mother patted her arm.

"He finally understands why no other relationship worked out, because there's only one person for him."

Willow reached for her champagne and took a drink to swallow the lump in her throat, but it refused to budge.

When the room fell silent, he finished. "You're my one, Willow. The more I know you, what a good person you are, the more I love you. You've made me the happiest man on the planet."

With that, he tossed the mic onto the table.

To prevent tears from escaping, she pressed her hands to her face. With purpose in each step, he strode toward her.

In front of everyone gathered to celebrate their union, Jax tugged her to her feet. Then, making her gasp with shock, he swept her off the floor and into his arms.

"You'll have to excuse us," he said to the crowd. "I'm taking my wife upstairs."

"Jax!" She kicked her legs helplessly. "You can't do this."

"Darling wife, I've waited long enough. If you want me to keep my hands off you until we're alone, you might want to stay still." His eyes were dark with promise.

She stopped squirming.

"Excellent choice." He summoned the elevator. "I meant what I said back there, Willow. I love you."

She exhaled. Part of her thought it was too soon. But the truth was, she felt it, too. And she knew that their commitment to each other would deepen their emotional connection. "I love you, too, Jax."

His smile melted her heart.

"Let's consummate this marriage."

About time. "Yes, Sir."

The guests cheered as Jax carried her into the waiting compartment and took her to their suite to claim her as his wife.

Keep reading for a sneak preview from Rafe Sterling's story, Billionaire's Matchmaker.

I hope you loved Jax as much as I do. Be sure to find out what's happening with Rafe Sterling in the Billionaire's Matchmaker. Suddenly he's a man in need of a bride. And his solution to the problem shocks his gorgeous matchmaker! I guarantee you a happily ever after with no cheating.

Be sure to check out the bestselling Bonds heroes, beginning with Crave.

Have you ever wanted to be Mastered? Here's your chance. Discover why With This Collar was a #1 best seller. Master Marcus will curl your toes and give you a very happily ever after.

Don't miss any news! Sign up for my VIP reader newsletter for updates, giveaways, bonus reads, and more.

Please connect with me on social media or drop me an email. I love hearing from you! www.sierracartwright.com.

Titans

An exclusive private society of the world's most powerful ambitious gentlemen

Hope Malloy is not intimidated by rich, powerful men. So when she's hired to find a bride for billionaire Rafe Sterling, she's certain the assignment will be easy. Not only is he sexy and a renowned philanthropist, the man is heir to one of the country's largest hotel fortunes. Who wouldn't want to marry him?

Rafe Sterling does not want a wife. Too bad it's the one thing he desperately needs. His father ran off with a woman half his age, and Rafe can't become permanent CEO of Sterling Worldwide unless he's married.

When he's ambushed by the competent matchmaker, he's captivated by her intelligence and seductive innocence.

All of a sudden, he is thinking about a future and having her under his complete and total command.

Will she run when she discovers his deepest, darkest secrets and shocking, sensual demands?

CHAPTER ONE

Rafe Sterling strode through the door of his downtown Houston office and into a Monday morning predawn ambush.

To make matters worse, his shoulder hurt from where he'd landed on it during a bicycle race the previous day, he'd slept badly, and he hadn't had a single cup of coffee.

Three women stood with their backs to the window, a terrifying army in silk and stilettos.

His mother, Rebecca, had her arms folded across her chest, wearing resolve like armor. His sister, Arianna, was in the middle, and she squirmed under his scrutiny. *Good.* At best, she was a reluctant accomplice.

The third woman, all the way on the right, he'd never met.

Her well-defined cheekbones were striking, and her lips were painted a wicked shade of fuck-me red. She wore her long brunette hair loose, the locks flowing around her shoulders. But it was the way she studied him, with total focus, that riveted his attention. Her eyes were a startling shade, not hazel but deeper, like gold. For a moment—a fascinating, unwanted, and mercifully brief flash of time—he imagined them swimming with tears of submission.

He cleared his throat, and she broke their connection by glancing toward the floor.

Fuck. Her gesture arrowed through his gut. For the first time in years—since Emma—he was captivated.

Rafe shook his head. He had no patience for relationships, not even with a woman who wore a skirt that hugged her enticing curves.

"Rafe, darling!" His mother broke ranks and took a couple of steps toward him.

Galvanized, he closed his office door behind him. Better to meet the battle head-on so he could get on with his day. "Morning, ladies."

He crossed the room to drop an obligatory kiss on his mother's cheek, then he noticed a pile of folders on his desk. Something to do with the visit from the unnamed woman, no doubt.

With distrust, he flicked another glance in her direction. Who the hell was she? "To what do I owe the pleasure of your company?" Rafe eased into his leather executive chair.

His mother took a seat across from him and skipped any further pretense of pleasantries. "You need a wife."

"Ah." He slid the manila menaces to the edge of the desk and resisted—barely—the urge to knock them into the waiting trash can. "Understood. Now this is the part of the confrontation where I tell you I will find a bride when I'm damn well ready. Thank you for your time and concern." He attempted a smile. Judging by his mother's wince, the curl of his lips was closer to a snarl. "I'm sure you can show yourselves out."

"Don't be rude, Rafael Barron Sterling."

He quirked an eyebrow. His mother hadn't used his full name since he was in college.

"Your father is planning to marry Elizabeth."

Rafe opened his mouth, then closed it without speaking. He didn't need to state the obvious. His parents were still married.

"It's imperative we make you the CEO of Sterling Worldwide. This madness must stop at once," Rebecca finished.

"Mother—"

"He bought her a forty-thousand-dollar ring. I saw a picture of it in his email. Gaudy. He has terrible judgment and even worse taste." She shoved the manila folders back to the center of the desk.

Because of Theodore's unstable behavior, his mother suspected her husband had the early stages of dementia. His physician disagreed, saying that Theodore was at an age where he'd acquired vast wealth and wanted to enjoy it. The motorcycles he couldn't ride and the yacht that needed a crew were proof of that, as were the classic Rolls Royce, a chauffeur, a château in France, and a twenty-three-year-old mistress to enjoy it with.

Rafe suspected that both his mother and the doctor were partially correct. Theodore had never wanted any part in Sterling Worldwide. He'd been the unexpected and much pampered late-in-life and third-born child of Barron and Penelope Sterling. His parents had believed Theodore to be nothing less than a gift from God, and they'd treated him as such, indulging his every whim, allowing him to travel the world from a young age, buying him gifts that had been denied to his siblings. He'd also bypassed the boarding schools that the other Sterling children had attended. But his parents had insisted on a college education. They'd made a sizable donation to the university's foundation to ensure he received passing grades. Surprising everyone, including himself, he'd excelled in business school.

When his older brother, Barron Sterling, Jr., had been killed in a hunting accident, Theodore had been thrust into the unwelcome role as heir and CEO of a worldwide hotel empire. He hadn't known that his much more qualified sister couldn't inherit the business. He'd hired attorneys, but in the end, the terms were absolute. Theodore had lost his freedom and his jet-setting lifestyle. Within weeks of his brother's burial, he was married to the formidable Rebecca, a woman his mother had selected.

Now that Rafe had proven himself competent as the conglomerate's Chief Financial Officer, Theodore had run away from his day-to-day responsibilities in favor of living the life he'd imagined.

Unaware or uncaring that her son hadn't responded, Rebecca continued. "Ms. Malloy"—she pointed to the brunette—"has compiled a list of suitable candidates for your consideration."

"Candidates?"

"To become your wife," Ms. Malloy clarified, taking over the meeting. She crossed the room toward him, her hips swaying and her peep-toe shoes sounding a tattoo that did evil things to his libido.

When she stopped near his desk, her scent reached him, lilacs and summer, a contrast to the darkness that hovered over his life.

"The list has been narrowed to five finalists for your consideration." Obviously she had no clue she was rearranging his brain cells. "Each of the ladies is qualified to be your wife. Of course, for your privacy, they only know certain things about you. A general description, the fact that you're an executive, that you live in Houston. The women have been interviewed and prescreened. We have nondisclosures on record, so any exchange of information will be confidential. Because time is of the essence, a mixer on Thursday or Friday would be most expeditious. If you prefer, we can arrange casual meetings, coffee or breakfast, perhaps lunch as you narrow your selection to three. From there we will be happy to set up dinners. That way you can get to know her before actual social events. We can make it appear like a whirlwind romance and—"

"Stop." He held up a hand and trapped her gaze. "Who the fuck are you?"

"I didn't realize that you weren't aware…" She glanced toward his mother, but Rebecca looked down to pluck a piece of lint from her skirt

Recovering, the brunette smiled. The gesture was quick, practiced, and polished—meant to impart confidence without being too familiar.

Irrationally, it—she—irritated the hell out of him.

"I beg your pardon. I'm Hope Malloy." She extended her hand. "It's a pleasure to meet you, Mr. Sterling."

He ignored her gesture. "I asked you a question."

As she dropped her arm, her smile vanished. When she spoke, her tone was more formal. "I own The Prestige Group. Celeste Fallon recommended my team to your mother."

"Team of…what?"

"We are an elite matchmaking service for the world's wealthiest, most discerning individuals. We understand that it's difficult for men such as yourself to meet appropriate—"

"You're a *matchmaker*? You stick your nose in other people's business for a living?" Stunned, Rafe swung his gaze toward his mother. "What the hell are you thinking?"

"Watch your tone."

"You've got thirty seconds before I throw all of you out."

"I know this is a shock, so I'll forgive your bad manners. Prestige will be discreet on this search. No one needs to know it's happening."

He stood and slammed his palms flat on the desk surface. "You hired them to find me a *wife*?" The killer-heeled woman was here to marry him off to some nameless woman to safeguard the Sterling empire?

"Celeste has assured me that Ms. Malloy is the best."

Of that, he had no doubt. Fallon and Associates was one of the world's most exclusive crisis management firms. For more than a hundred and fifty years, they'd specialized in high-profile cases, restoring reputations, saving careers, ensuring people never talked. Like Sterling Worldwide, the Fallons had also kept the business private, and all owners had been related to the founder, Walter Fallon—who'd been part of a secret society at the University of Virginia with Rafe's great-great-great-great-grandfather, John.

Along with five other young men who'd been in the same organization, John and Walter had become lifelong friends. Over the years, the Sterlings and

Fallons had helped each other numerous times, including earlier in the year when Theodore and Lillibet had been caught in the first-class toilet of a commercial aircraft.

Thanks to Fallon and Associates, the investigation had gone away, and Celeste had managed to kill the story before a prominent East Coast newspaper could get anyone to verify the distasteful rumors.

As it was, only one blog had run the story, under the headline, *Little Girl and her Teddy Join the Mile High Club!* The teaser, as vile as it was provocative, had been a clever play on his father's name and the ridiculous age difference between the lovers.

A week later, the website had vanished.

"Ms. Malloy has done a fine job. At this rate, we can announce your engagement within a few weeks."

"Goodbye."

Undaunted, his mother went on. "It's a matter of time before your father causes a disaster we can't recover from." Even though anger strung her words together, she didn't raise her voice. As always, Rebecca was the picture of calm, focused resolve. "You're over thirty. If you had done your duty years ago, we wouldn't be facing this situation now."

He winced at the truth of the accusation. Ever since Rafe was a child, his mother had been clear about his obligations. But to him, love equaled drama, and he despised both.

"You need to be sensible." She brought her index fingers together and studied him.

Arianna joined them. "I know you don't like people meddling in your life, but—"

"Meddling?" He'd had enough. "You call this *meddling*?"

"Things are going to get worse, not better, with Dad and his—" Arianna caught her bottom lip with her teeth. "With Elizabeth."

Every day, Rafe hoped his father would return to Houston and his office, but since his dad and Lillibet, as he called her, had been ensconced in their St. Pete's Beach love nest for two weeks, that didn't seem imminent.

Rafe sighed. "I know you're concerned, and I understand it." More than ready to get out of this mess, he said, "I'll talk to him again."

"You've done so numerous times," Rebecca pointed out.

Dozens. Maybe more. "If necessary, I'll fly out there."

"What if it doesn't work?" Rebecca asked in a chilled tone. "This cannot continue. You're a smart man, Rafe. You know how delicate this situation is. Let's not make it any more complicated than it needs to be."

Possible scenarios lined up in his mind and fired across his brain in a burst of nightmares, each worse than the last. Theodore asking for a divorce. His mother being awarded half of the company and the courts being involved in the painstaking divisions. It could drag on for years while his father played with his mistress. In a worst-case situation, Theodore might, indeed, commit bigamy, which would create a public relations quagmire that Sterling Worldwide might not recover from.

Rafe pinched the bridge of his nose.

"Noah stopped by the house Friday evening," Rebecca said. "Your father isn't returning calls. I understand from his assistant that Noah's been dropping by the executive office every day. She's been making excuses, but she isn't convinced he believes her."

Rafe struggled to hold his temper in check. His cousin, Noah Richardson, son of Rafe's aunt, Victoria Sterling-Richardson, believed he had grounds to challenge Rafe's position as heir apparent. According to the archaic terms of the trust, succession went to male descendants in birth order. Even then, the heir was required to be married.

Noah ran one of the divisions, was a multimillionaire in his own right, and he believed he was the rightful heir since Rebecca and Theodore hadn't been married when Barron, Jr., had been killed. Noah itched to break up the corporation and sell it off, a philosophy Rafe was against. Noah had threatened to see Rafe in court numerous times. Rafe had responded that any challenge should have come a generation ago. But because Noah was married with children, there was a chance, however slight, that he might prevail in a court case. Even if the decision was in Rafe's favor, the litigation could drag on for months, even years. The financial cost could be devastating.

"I'm sorry." Arianna wrung her hands. "I hate this, and I didn't want to be part of it. It's awful that we have to coerce you into doing something you're not ready to do."

He believed her. Unlike him, she was a romantic, a dreamer shattered by her second divorce.

"Arianna and I will leave you to it." Rebecca stood.

"I haven't agreed to anything." He refused to be railroaded.

"You'll do what you need to." His mother wasn't backing down.

She closed the door with a decisive *click*, sealing him in with the enemy. Hope was a beautiful, seductive temptress, but the enemy, nonetheless.

"You're a matchmaker."

"It's an honorable profession."

"Is it? Much like operating an escort service. I hire you. I will end up paying to fuck a woman, one who's interchangeable with any number of other *candidates*."

"That's as insulting as it is crass." She set her chin and didn't sever the connection of their gazes, meeting the heat of his anger with cool, aloof professionalism.

He wanted to shake it from her, strip her bare, discover what lay beneath the surface to leave nothing but aching, pulsing honesty between them.

Either not noticing the tension or ignoring it, she continued. "Throughout history, families arranged marriages all the time. In parts of the world, it still goes on. Today, there's a bigger need for my services than ever before. I have clients all over the world, from all sorts of backgrounds and of all ages. Often, men in your position don't have time to meet women in the traditional way. You're far too busy, important, insulated."

"Spare me the sales pitch."

"It makes sense to select someone I've interviewed, a woman who suits the needs of a man such as you. A woman of the right temperament, with the same interests, goals, morals, outlook, political leanings, religious preferences. A woman who understands what is expected of her and is willing to assume those responsibilities."

"A business arrangement."

"If you like."

Rafe took his seat and left her standing. It was undoubtedly rude, but justified. His mother had hired Prestige, but Hope had been part of the early-morning intervention. She could have refused, but she hadn't. That made her complicit. "So that's what's in here?" He flicked a glance at the folders. "A money-hungry bride-to-be—I beg your pardon, *candidate*—who understands what she's getting herself into?"

"These women all deserve your respect."

"And an expensive engagement ring?" He leaned back. "Why should I trust you?"

"Five years of success. Thirty-seven marriages."

"Divorces?"

"Two."

"Much better than the national average. Yet five years in business means your experiment hasn't made it to the seven-year itch yet."

"Whether that exists or not is a matter of debate. There's a study that suggests there's a four-year itch as well as a seven-year one. Oh, and a three-year one. And most couples who divorce tend to do so after a decade. So that means there's a twelve-year flameout as well." She lifted one delicate shoulder in a half shrug. "Whatever your bias, you can find a study to support it. The truth is, each individual is unique, and so are their relationships. People divorce for a lot of reasons and after any length of time."

"Fair enough."

"There are, however, a number of factors that enhance chances for success. I call them the Three C's — compatibility, chemistry, and commitment."

"Define success."

She tipped her head to one side. "I suppose that's in the eye of the beholder."

"Take my parents. They've been victims of wedded bliss for thirty-three years."

"There are financial and legal benefits for people who are married."

She'd sidestepped his point neatly.

"Couples who are wed, versus those who cohabitate, tend to live longer."

"Or perhaps it only seems that way."

She smiled, and it transformed her features, making her no longer standoffish and professional, but warm and inviting. No wonder lemmings turned to her for matrimonial advice. "Have you always been a cynic, Mr. Sterling?"

"About marriage?" *Not always.* But the few illusions he'd held had been shattered. "Can you blame me?"

"You can't think of any positive examples?"

"Like my sister? She's twenty-seven and going through her second divorce, and this one is more gruesome and costly than the first. My best friend and college roommate, Griffin Lahey? His wife of three years just walked out, dumped him, ripped apart their future, and took away their son. For the final knife in his heart, she's suing for half of his estate because she met an artist who she fancies and wants to move to Paris with him. Noah's parents live on separate continents. My grandmother had to be coaxed into attending my grandfather's funeral. I'm told she was drunk at the time, and not from grief. On the morning he was to be buried, legend has it that she knocked back an entire bottle of champagne...from the private reserve he had saved for special occasions. So, no, I'm not anxious to stick my neck in the matrimonial noose."

"You asked why you should trust me. You shouldn't. You have no reason to, yet. I could give you references from satisfied customers. I could reassure you that I've signed a nondisclosure. Or that Celeste Fallon believes in me. But none of that means anything. You need results. If the potential women I've matched you with don't suit your needs, I'll give you another five. Or fire me and I'll refund your mother's fee."

"Fee?" He narrowed his eyes. "How much do you charge?"

"I'm expensive, Mr. Sterling."

"Ten thousand dollars? Twenty?" When she didn't react, he tried again. "More than that?"

"A hundred thousand."

"Shit." People were willing to pay a hundred grand to meet someone? If it worked out, he'd have the honor of shelling out thousands more for baubles to go along with it? Then, when the shine wore off, she'd keep them *and* half his fortune?

"I'm worth every penny."

"That's pretty confident."

"I am." She folded her arms across her chest. "I work hard to ensure I satisfy my clients."

He glanced at the top folder as if it were rabid. "How did you choose these particular women?"

"In normal circumstances, I meet with a gentleman so I can get a sense about him. Then he fills in a questionnaire. It's rather detailed. Fourteen pages of likes, dislikes, things that worked in previous relationships. Things that didn't."

"Go on."

"Expectations around traditions are important as are roles in the relationship. To some, religion is important. I find out if he wants children. If so, how many? Will he want them raised in a particular religion? Where does he plan to live? In the US or abroad? Will the children attend private school?

Boarding school? Will a nanny be hired? A housekeeper? After I've reviewed that, I have a second meeting with him for further clarification."

"And they need you for this?"

"Most of the men I work with don't have the opportunity to meet women they might be serious about marrying. They've often focused their attention on their careers or education. Some of them are famous, but they don't want to settle down with a woman they've met on the road or someone who's been part of their fan club."

"And where do you find the women who are anxious to throw themselves at the feet of these rich men?"

"I belong to a number of organizations, and I'm active in Houston's art and business communities. It may surprise you, but I'm often invited to high-society events. I've seen you at a few."

Rafe regarded her again. "We haven't met." He would have remembered. Her eyes, her voice, the sweet curve of her hips, the way her legs went on forever in those shoes. Yeah. He would have remembered.

"No. I spend most of my time talking with women. Part of my value is that I've met all the candidates, interviewed them, watched them interact at social events." She nudged a folder toward him. "Try me."

"Have a seat." Rafe wondered at his sudden offer of hospitality. He didn't need Hope and her lilac-and-silk scent in his office while he looked through the files.

She sat opposite him, her movements delicate. Her skirt rode up her bare thighs, just a bit. He imagined skimming his fingers across her smooth skin while she gasped, then yanking down her panties, curving his fingers into the hot flesh of her ass cheeks.

Christ. He'd spent all Saturday working on next quarter's business plan. In the previous day's bike race against some of his friends, he'd pushed too fast, too hard, on a grueling part of the course and crashed. He'd had a shot of Crown before going to bed but skipped taking anything else for the pain. He'd slept like hell, and he'd spent too long working out cramps in the shower to even think about masturbating.

Now, he wished he had taken the edge off.

It had been over a month since he'd visited the Retreat, a BDSM club in a historic warehouse on Buffalo Bayou in downtown Houston, and even longer since he'd enjoyed the singular pleasure of playing with a sub at the discreet second-story Quarter in New Orleans. Of course being this close to an attractive female after such an intense drought would give him an erection. *Shit.* He couldn't force himself to believe his own fucking lie. Every day, he was surrounded by beautiful women. He wanted Hope. With her ass upturned, listening to her frantic breaths as she waited for his belt...waited for his touch. It was more than the sound of her voice or the innocent-yet-provocative shoes, it was carnal desire. Lust. The last time he was gripped by its power, he'd been in college and far more helpless than he was now.

He imprisoned his thoughts and focused on the task in front of him.

Picking up the first file, he flipped it open.

The top page had a name, a picture, and the vital statistics of a beautiful twenty-four-year-old blonde. She was a UT Austin graduate, a pageant winner who flashed a tiara-worthy smile and worked as a fundraiser for underprivileged schools.

In every way, on paper, she should interest him. She was attractive, knew how to handle herself in public, and she had philanthropic inclinations.

Naturally his mother would approve. And yet... He felt nothing—less than nothing. He was uninspired and disinterested. The hard-on he'd been sporting vanished. He glanced up at Hope Malloy. "You said chemistry matters?"

"She doesn't appeal to you?"

"Not in the least."

"Perhaps you'll have better luck with another choice?"

He didn't.

After perusing the second picture, he glanced back at Hope.

"Nothing?"

"No."

"It's possible the attraction would develop after you meet someone. Her choice of conversation, the way she moves or looks at you." She shifted. "Pheromones."

Those, he was starting to believe in. Keeping his mind on the folders, he said, "I see. My mother hopes I will select a bride, whether I want to fuck her or not?"

Hot pink scorched Hope's cheekbones before she recovered. "So, you would rather have a spine-tingling attraction to someone who consumes you?"

"No." He'd had that. Once. With Emma, in college. He'd been crazy enough about her that he'd bought her a stunning ring.

He had been invited to join her family for Christmas brunch, and he'd intended to propose then. Unbeknownst to him, Emma had been so intent on getting married that she'd been juggling dates with three different men. One of them had popped the question on Christmas Eve in front of the tree's twinkling lights.

When she'd called to let him know, she wasn't apologetic. She reminded him she wanted a wedding as a college graduation present, and Aaron had offered her just that. It was nothing personal. She would have been happy marrying any of them.

Rafe had hit the local bar near a shopping center. When he left, there'd been a red kettle set up outside. A man nearby was ringing a bell and asking for charitable donations. Rafe stuffed her ring through the slot and accepted the candy the bell ringer offered as thanks.

A sucker. If there'd ever been a more appropriate gesture, he didn't recall it.

Rafe had spent every day until the new year in an alcohol-induced stupor, calling her at all hours, sending desperate text messages, even driving to her home in a stupid and embarrassing attempt to get her to change her mind.

"Mr. Sterling?" Hope's questioning voice cut through the morose memories.

He flipped the folder closed without reading any of the pages. He refused to be out of control over a woman ever again. But if he was expected to marry and produce an heir or two, he should at least want to go to bed with her.

"Perhaps of the three C's, compatibility and commitment are more important than chemistry?"

How much longer until he could dismiss her?

When he didn't answer, she filled the silence. "Can you tell me what it was about the first two candidates that didn't suit your needs? It will help me refine the search."

"Ms. Malloy…" He struggled to leash his raging impatience. "Show some fucking mercy, will you? Until ten minutes ago, I didn't know I needed a *candidate.*"

She edged the third folder toward him.

With great reluctance but with a sudden urge to get through this, he thumbed it open. Another blonde. Another perfect smile. Another impeccable pedigree. "Since I didn't fill in your forms, I assume it was my mother who decided what college degrees and background were important?"

"Your sister rounded it out as far as activities you enjoy."

"Yet I don't see any of them who like to ride a mountain bike."

"Not a huge demand in this part of Texas."

"Kayaking?"

"I'll add that to the next search."

He gave in to curiosity. "Was Celeste consulted?"

"I invited her to be part of process. She declined."

If Celeste had been involved, perhaps there would have been a redhead or a brunette. Even someone with pink toenails in peekaboo shoes.

For the second time, he resisted the impulse to hurl the files in the trash. Instead, he opened his top drawer and swept the offensive lot inside, then slammed it shut.

Hope uncrossed her legs and leaned toward him. Then, evidently thinking better of it, she sat back and recrossed them.

He swore her skin whispered like the promise of sin.

"Perhaps you should consider the options at a more convenient time," she suggested.

"I'll see you receive full payment." He stood.

"I've already received it."

His mother had written this woman a check for a hundred grand? "Thank you for your efforts."

"Mr. Sterling—"

He walked past her to the door and opened it.

She sighed but stood. After gathering her purse—a small pink thing shaped like a cat, complete with ears and whiskers—she joined him. Instead of leaving, as he'd ordered, she stood in front of him, chin tipped at a defiant angle.

Hope projected competence, but the heels and fanciful handbag gave her a feminine air. A sane man would think of her as a vendor or business associate, so he could slot her into the *off-limits* part of his conscience. She wasn't a potential date or wife. Or submissive.

He wanted her.

She isn't mine.

Fuck his conscience.

Before this ridiculous idea about finding him a woman to marry went any further, she needed to know the truth about him, the side he locked away and kept hidden unless he was at one of his favorite BDSM clubs, the side that Celeste should have informed his matchmaker about.

Bare inches separated him from Hope, and he halved that distance by leaning toward her. "Is there a place on your fourteen-page questionnaire to discuss sexual proclivities?"

"I'm not sure what you mean." Her knuckles whitened on her purse strap.

"Let me clarify." Rafe spoke softly into the thick air between them. "Kinks. Those nasty, scandalous things that people do in the privacy of their own homes. Things they don't talk about in public. Salacious acts that make them drop to their knees in church as they beg forgiveness. Would you consider that compatibility or chemistry?"

Tension tightened her shoulders. "Is there something…" Her tone suggested she was trying for professionalism, but her voice cracked on a sharp inhalation.

After a few more shallow breaths, she ventured, "What do I need to know?"

"I'm into BDSM."

Her beautiful, pouty mouth parted a little.

An image scorched him—that of him slipping a spider gag between her lips, spreading her mouth and keeping it that way. He'd force her to communicate with her expression and her body, like she was now. "Your eyes are wide, Ms. Malloy. Are you shocked? Interested?" Her soul was reflected in the startling depths. "Curious, perhaps?"

It took her less than three seconds to close her mouth and regroup. "No. I'm wondering how I should phrase this for your candidates."

She'd lied. Instead of meeting his gaze, she stared at the potted plant near the window.

Rather than unleashing the beast that suddenly wanted to dominate her, he kept his tone even. "I'm sure you've had clients who like that sort of thing?"

Finally, after a breath, she looked at him. "I'll make some discreet inquiries of the candidates. What is it you're looking for?"

He ached to capture her chin and force her to look at him. "How much do you know about BDSM?"

She pulled back her shoulders, as if on more stable ground. "I've heard of it."

"No personal experience?"

"That's not relevant."

Damn her dishonest answer. Some? None? Would he be her first? Could he take her, mold her into what he wanted?

What the fuck was wrong with him? He'd already decided she was off-limits. "There are as many ways to practice BDSM as there are people in the lifestyle. No relationship is the same."

"Makes sense."

Mesmerized, he watched the wild flutter of her pulse in her throat. It was like oxygen to a dying man. He wanted more. "Some people prefer to confine their practices to the bedroom—at night, for example. Others, on occasion, indulge at a club or play party. A number of people practice it in varying degrees on a twenty-four-hour basis."

"Where do your...proclivities lie?"

Until now, he hadn't considered he might want a submissive wife. Over the years, he'd found it easier to go to the club. He was a Dom who would give a sub what she wanted, whether it was pain, roleplay, humiliation, a sensuous flogging, hours with torturous toys.

When he'd planned to marry Emma, he assumed she would work at a job that inspired her.

Alternatively, she'd have been free to engage in social activities or charity endeavors like the wives of some of his associates. Giving up his clubs hadn't been a consideration. Nor had he allowed himself to think of calling his bride at five p.m. and telling her to meet him in the foyer of his loft, naked, with her thighs spread and cunt shaved.

Now, however, he couldn't banish the thought. And since his mother had already squandered a hundred grand, he figured he should be specific in his requests. More, he wanted Hope to know what she was getting into, even if she didn't yet realize he'd chosen her. "I want my wife to be submissive twenty-four hours a day."

"Can you clarify what you mean?" She clenched the handle of her kitty bag, seeming to pretend this was an ordinary conversation with a normal man.

Jeanine, the best executive assistant on the continent, entered the outer office. She'd been with Sterling Worldwide for almost thirty years, and with him for the past seven. With her polite smile and firm voice, she protected him against the world. "Morning, Mr. Sterling."

"Jeanine."

She angled her head toward Hope. "Everything all right, sir?"

"Unscheduled meeting with the Prestige Group."

"I see."

"My mother arranged it."

Jeanine scowled with understanding. Like a she-dragon, Jeanine would have protected him from his own mother. "Anything you need, Mr. Sterling?" She was asking if he wanted her to call security or to show the woman out. "Coffee?"

Her combination of savviness and loyalty made her indispensable.

"Just one cup, please. Ms. Malloy won't be staying."

He captured Hope's shoulders and pulled her into his office so he could close the door. He held on to her for a whole lot longer than was necessary but not as long as he wanted to. How would she react if he eased his first finger up the delicate column of her throat?

Would she surrender? Fight the inevitable?

Forcing himself to resist the driving impulse, he dropped his hands and curled them into fists at his sides.

"Proclivities," she prompted.

The word echoed in his head. "She'll wear a collar—my collar..." And because he could no longer resist, he traced an index finger across the hollow of her throat. Her pulse fluttered, and her breaths momentarily ceased. "My woman will know that she belongs to me and she will behave as such."

Hope's gaze remained locked on his. When she spoke, her voice wobbled. "And this...collar. She'll have to wear it all the time?"

"That's what twenty-four seven means." A devilish grin tugged at his lips. He kept his fingertip pressed to her warm skin. "It will be subtle, however. Nothing gaudy. Unless people knew, I doubt they'd think she was wearing anything other than a striking piece of jewelry. But her play collar, the one she wears in private with me or at a lifestyle event, may be different."

"Like at a BDSM club or something?" She nodded, as if she were on ground she understood.

Not that he'd let her stay there long. "I enjoy showing off my sub. There's a certain restaurant in New Orleans, Vieille Rivière, that she will go to. And she'll join me when I visit people in similar social circles." *Including other Titans.* But there was a limit to how much he should tell her. "There are certain things I would want her to go along with. Bondage. Sensory deprivation."

"You mean like blindfolds and handcuffs?" There was no hesitation in her words, so he ascertained she'd made sense of what he'd said and decided that fell under the category of typical bedroom shenanigans.

"Among others, yes. I use blindfolds on occasion. I like gags so that my woman must beg with her eyes. Her tears are like dripping nectar from the gods."

Wide-eyed, uncertain, she sucked in a deep, disbelieving breath.

"Clamps," he added, skimming the column of her throat.

"I…"

"On her nipples, among other places. And I will want to her to wait for me at the end of a long day, on her knees, head tipped back, her beautiful mouth held open by a dental dam."

"You mean…she'd have to do this herself?"

"Prepare for my homecoming?" He imagined Hope parting her lips, sliding in the dam and positioning it, pictured her naked in front of the door, hungry for his touch. "Yes."

She retreated a step. "Mr. Sterling, I—"

"My wife will focus on me and my pleasure."

"That sounds rather old-fashioned."

"Does it? What you're not aware of is what I'm willing to do in return."

"In return?"

"I wouldn't expect a woman to give me everything she has to offer without me giving equal parts of myself. Her wants and desires will be my highest priority. I will give her the heavens if she wants them, the stars, the moon." He paused. "Then I'll take her to the depths of hell as she uncovers what sets her depraved soul free."

She shuddered.

"Can you find me all that in a *candidate*, Ms. Malloy?"

"You're rather particular."

"Indeed. I require a woman of impeccable breeding who presents her ass for my punishment when she displeases me."

The air conditioner kicked on. The whispering cool air did nothing to dissipate the heat between them.

He slid his hand around to the back of her neck, then feathered his fingers into her hair. "I want to kiss you, Ms. Malloy."

"Uhm…"

"Ask me to."

She scowled.

"I won't have you pretending that you're not curious. When you're at home this evening, by yourself with a glass of wine, horny and considering masturbating—"

"That's not me." She shook her head so fast it was obviously a desperate lie.

"No? Ms. Malloy, the room is swimming with your pheromones. Deny it." She sagged a little against his hand, and he tightened his grip on her hair, as much to offer support as to imprison her. Then he continued as if she hadn't interrupted. "You'll remember this moment, fantasize about being mine."

"No…"

"Invite me to kiss you or tell me to release you. The power is yours. Yield to temptation or leave this room wondering if it's as good as you imagine it will be."

"Mr. Sterling, this can't be happening."

Despite her protest, she didn't try to escape. "I agree. This is the first time I've had three women"—four if he counted Celeste—"attempt to force me

137

down the aisle." He paused. "And it's the first time I've had this kind of sexual longing for an adversary. Ask me to kiss you," he repeated instead of arguing. "Be sure to say please."

"Ah…"

He loosened his grip, and she leaned toward him, keeping herself hostage. Rafe didn't smile with triumph.

"Kiss me."

"There's nothing I'd enjoy more." That wasn't the entire truth. There were a hundred things he'd like to do to her, but he made no move

Her internal standoff lasted longer than he thought it would. Excellent. She had a stubborn streak.

Hope glanced away and sighed. Then she looked at him with clear, confident eyes. "Please kiss me."

He could drown in her and be happy about it. He captured her chin to hold her steady. On her lips, he tasted the sweetness of her capitulation. "Open your mouth, sweet Hope."

She did, and he entered her mouth, slower than he would ordinarily, softer than he would if she were his submissive.

Hope responded with hesitation, and he continued, driving deeper, seeking more. Within seconds, she yielded.

She moaned and raised onto her tiptoes to lean into him. A few seconds beyond that, she wrapped her arms around him. Hope, his adversary, had now become his willing captive.

He released her chin and moved his hand to the middle of her back, then lower to the base of her spine.

Rafe drank in the scent of her femininity. His cock surged, not from ordinary arousal, but from soul-deep recognition. Her eagerness sought the Dom in him. It took all his restraint not to press his palm against her buttocks.

Earlier he'd said she'd be thinking of him as she masturbated. The truth was, he wasn't sure how he'd banish this memory of her—strength and suppleness in one heady package.

He plundered her mouth.

She offered more until she was panting and desperate, gripping him hard.

Instead of giving in to the driving need to rip off her clothes and fuck her, he distracted himself by tugging on her hair harder. As he'd requested, her eyes were open. *So goddamn trusting.* Did she have any idea how close he was to shredding the veneer of civilization that hung between them to claim her, mark her as his?

He ended the kiss while he still could. Her mouth was swollen, and he couldn't stop staring at her lips.

Hope took tiny breaths that didn't seem to steady her. She held on to him while she lowered her heels to the floor. Then, over a few heartbeats, she dropped her hands.

"Thank you, Rafe," he prompted.

"Are you serious? I'm supposed to thank you?" She continued to look at him and undoubtedly saw his resolve.

Would she give him what he demanded? "Unless you want me to spank—"

"Spank?" Her chin was at a full tilt.

"Spank." He repeated with emphasis. "Unless you want me to spank your pretty little ass so hard that you can't sit down after you leave here."

"That kind of behavior is unacceptable."

"Under normal circumstances," he agreed without hesitation. "Unless you ask me for it." Part of him hoped she'd take him up on it. It would be a pleasure to prove she liked the feel of his hand on her bare skin. "I'll go first." He softened his tone, letting her glimpse his inner thoughts, a rare confession of his soul. "I enjoyed kissing you. Thank you."

"I…" She smoothed the skirt that he wanted to rip off her body.

"Look at me."

She followed his command. Then, with a soft and decidedly insubmissive tone, she said, "Thank you."

"Ms. Malloy, as I said, it was my pleasure."

Silence hung between them. Her inexperience thrilled him, and he wanted to give her another hundred firsts. Instead, he let her go. The real world—with its complex demands—was waiting. And if he wanted her at his feet, he had a lot of work to do.

"I'm not certain how much of what you said, and what we just did, is to get me to admit defeat, to quit..." She stiffened her spine.

"Maybe it started that way." His father's behavior had pissed Rafe off, and so had his mother's ambush, even Hope herself. He'd wanted to shake her as badly as he'd been shaken. As he'd spoken to her, his desires had churned to the surface. Until now—until *her*—he had been willing to confine his kink to a club. "It didn't end that way. That I promise you."

"I will ask the candidates about their openness to your suggestions."

Fuck. She wanted to retreat behind a facade of business, as if their kiss hadn't changed something. "Requirements. Not suggestions. Requirements. Be clear about that. If I'm to be saddled with a woman that I don't want until death do us part, there will be none of the hysteria that my family members seem to thrive on. My *wife* will know her place and her role, and she will meet my expectations. And to be clear, she *will* ask for my kiss. Like you did." He opened the door.

Jeanine was walking toward his office with a cup of coffee, and he waved her off.

Then, voice so soft that only Hope could hear, he finished. "You have a fourteen-page interview form. I will have something similar for the women you bring to me. It will cover things such as anal play, being shared with others, edging, exhibitionism. Shall I send it to you first?"

"Please do. It will save some time in your selection process." She started past him, and he snagged her elbow.

"And Ms. Malloy? She'll fucking address me as Sir." He was unaccountably furious at her rejection. At himself. "And if you come here ever again, so will you."

Her hand trembled where she grasped her purse strap. She flicked a glance at his hand before yanking her elbow free and continuing.

She paused at Jeanine's desk to say goodbye. Why did that matter so much to him?

He should have snagged the cup of coffee and returned to his office to call his father, but Rafe continued to watch Hope. Each damnable step made her hips sway, and his still-hard cock throbbed in response.

At the door leading to the hallway, Hope paused, her hand on the knob. She glanced over her shoulder and met his gaze without blinking. He might have unsettled her, even shocked her. But he hadn't scared her.

Round one to the beautiful matchmaker.

Available at most book retailers.

OTHER TITLES BY SIERRA CARTWRIGHT

Titans

Sexiest Billionaire
Billionaire's Matchmaker
Billionaire's Christmas

Power

His to Claim
His to Cherish

Bonds

Crave
Claim
Command

The Donovans

Bind
Brand
Boss

Mastered

With This Collar
On His Terms
Over The Line
In His Cuffs

For The Sub
In The Den

Master Class

Initiation
Enticement

Hawkeye

Come to Me
Trust in Me
Meant for Me

Individual titles

Double Trouble
Shockwave
Bound and Determined
Three-Way Tie
Signed, Sealed, and Delivered

ABOUT SIERRA CARTWRIGHT

Sierra Cartwright was born in England, and her early childhood was spent traipsing through castles and dreaming of happily-ever afters. She was raised in the Wild West and now lives in Galveston, Texas. She loves the beach and the artistic vibe of the island.